Lovers
Restored

a Lovers Redeemed novel

Kelsie Leverich

D1520716

Entangled Publishing, LLC
2614 South Timberline Road
Suite 109
Fort Collins, CO 80525
Visit our website at www.entangledpublishing.com.

Brazen is an imprint of Entangled Publishing, LLC. For more information on our titles, visit www.brazenbooks.com.

Edited by Stephen Morgan
Cover design by Heather Howland
Photography by Nikki Rae

Manufactured in the United States of America

First Edition November 2014

Chapter One

Halle Morgan parked beneath the old sign hanging in front of Gina's Diner and cut the engine. It'd been ten years since she'd stepped foot in Glenley, Indiana, and why she found herself in front of the diner of all places she wasn't sure. For the ice cream? She would've laughed if she wasn't so freaked out.

If she left now, she could be back in Columbus before midnight. No harm done. The idea settled around her like a security blanket.

No. She couldn't leave. Not yet. She had to fulfill the pact she'd made with her best friend ten years ago.

Then she was out of here.

With an encouraging breath, she left the solace of her car and stepped onto the sidewalk in front of the diner. The windows were covered with green and white paint, congratulating the graduating senior class and boasting their Gator pride. There was a moment in time when she'd loved this town. After all, she'd grown up here. Glenley was one of those small, stagnant towns where football was life, and gossip spread as fast as the word of God.

She could only imagine the whispers if anyone realized she was back.

It felt like a lifetime ago that she walked through the high school with her best friend Peyton at her side, both of them wearing their caps and gowns. Nothing to worry about other than what to wear, what graduation party to attend first, and who was going to drive to the next town over and use a fake ID to get beer for the weekend.

They'd thought they were invincible. Turned out they'd been wrong.

She shook the thought from her mind and walked inside the diner. The pleasant aroma of juicy burgers and hand cut French fries filled her nose, the smell drifting her attention back to the present. She hadn't realized how hungry she was until then.

She glanced around. Everything looked just as she recalled. Cracked vinyl booths atop green linoleum floors were surrounded by the occasional table for two. And though it was dated, she was glad to see it hadn't changed.

She moved to the counter at the deep end of the diner and sat down. "Hi."

"Hi," the teenage girl behind the counter said, handing her a menu. "Can I get you anything to drink while you decide what you'd like?"

Using the foot ledge beneath the counter for balance, she shifted on her barstool and tried to balance her purse on her lap. The barstools were just as uncomfortable as they were ten years ago. Yet, somehow, that in and of itself was comforting.

She skimmed the menu, as familiar as her dad's famous S'more building instructions. Graham cracker, peanut butter, burnt marshmallow, Twix candy bar, graham cracker. Then dipped in honey.

A smiled eased across her face. "You know what? I'll take a large bowl of vanilla ice cream. But can you crumble pretzels on top and load it with hot fudge and pineapple?"

She hadn't had her favorite concoction in years. No matter how many times she'd tried to duplicate it, she'd never quite gotten it right. Nothing compared to Gina's homemade ice cream, and she'd kill for the recipe.

The young girl's brows knitted together, and she gave Halle an amused smile. "Um, sure."

"Oh," Halle blurted as the waitress started to turn away. "And can you bring me a side of fries for dipping?"

The girl laughed. "You got it."

Halle began digging in her purse for her phone. It wasn't particularly like her to check up on her employees, but then again, she'd never had to. Ever since she'd opened Pink Pepper Catering with her friend, Courtney, a few years back, she'd always been there for every event. Graduation season was second to wedding season, so needless to say, they were swamped.

Considering how much she hated being included in group texts, she felt a little guilty as she pressed the send button.

Halle: Hi guys. How are preparations for Friday's events going?

It didn't take long for the first few responses to pop up.

Tessa: Not so good. We lost the order for the Frick graduation party.

Brian: The main oven died. Down to the back up.

Lauren: I quit.

Halle rolled her eyes and smiled. Perfect example of why she hated group texts. But she loved her team. She should've known they'd give her a hard time.

Halle: Funny. Let me guess, Courtney put you up to it?

Radio silence.

She was just about to send another message when a single text from Courtney came in.

Courtney: You make it?

Halle: Yep. Just got here, actually. Please tell me my oven didn't really die.

Courtney: Your oven is fine. Now stop worrying about us. I've got everything covered.

Halle sighed. She wasn't worried, not about the events at least. But thinking about work was a lot safer than thinking about *him*. Who, quite frankly, she hadn't been able to stop thinking about since her tires rolled through town. No. That wasn't entirely true. If she was being completely honest with herself, she hadn't stopped thinking about him in ten years.

The phone buzzed in her hand, and she glanced back at the screen, grateful for the distraction.

Courtney: You okay?

She didn't know whether to tell her the truth or lie. Knowing Courtney, she was bound to get an earful either way she went.

"Here ya go," the waitress said, setting a heaping bowl in front of her. "Vanilla ice cream with pretzels, hot fudge, pineapple, and a side of fries. Would you like whip cream?" she asked, holding up a can of Reddi-wip.

Halle: I'm getting ready to dig in to a bowl of ice cream. Couldn't be better.

She dropped her phone back in her purse, hoping her texts appeased Courtney…for now.

"Whip cream? No way, that'll ruin it."

"Okay, let me know if I can get you anything else." Halle watched as the young girl went googly-eyed as she glanced past Halle's shoulder before retreating to the kitchen.

Halle overflowed her spoon with yummy goodness and took a bite. "Mmm." Just like she remembered.

"Halle?" a voice said from behind her. It was gruff and deep, and it caused her insides to somersault.

Her hand stilled in front of her mouth, his words switching on the proverbial light bulb in her head. That voice?

No way. Not possible. No, no, no, no, no.

Karma wasn't that big of a bitch, was she?

Halle recited a silent prayer, hoping this wasn't who she thought it was. Please don't let it be *him*…please…

But according to the flutters in her chest, and her heated skin, Karma was laughing right now.

Slowly, she swiveled to face him and was met by a set of blue eyes she couldn't forget even if she tried.

Cooper Bale. Peyton's older brother.

She swore the air thickened between them. What was that saying? You never forget your first love? Though seeing him now, she almost wished she could.

The moment he sucked in a tight breath, she knew he recognized her. Her body was having its own mini meltdown as he stared at her; her pulse began to race, and the nerves she'd always felt around him returned with vengeance.

"Halle," he said, and there was no mistaking the shock and disappointment in his voice.

She tried to swallow the venom that had accumulated in her mouth. "Cooper."

Five minutes in this town and her worst fear had materialized in front of her. He was the last person she wanted to see. He was the reason she'd left Glenley in the first place. And looking at him now, it was obvious he still hated her.

She understood the why behind his anger. After all, she was the reason his little sister was dead. But no matter how hard she tried, the broken parts inside her couldn't see past the things he'd said to her all those years ago.

Shoving his hands in the front pockets of his jeans, he looked every bit as pained as she felt. He was broader, jaw chiseled and scruffy, his sandy hair longer. But up close, she could see exhaustion creasing his eyes. She hated the impulse that overcame her to throw her arms around his waist and soothe the ache that was etched into his once easy features.

Suddenly, she felt like she was eighteen again, lusting over her best friend's older brother—the man who encompassed the heart-shattering memory of the single night they'd shared together—shy and vulnerable and insecure in his presence.

But she wasn't that eighteen-year-old girl anymore; she was a grown woman now. She could handle this.

"What are you doing here?" he asked.

Deep breath, Halle, deep breath.

She gestured toward her bowl. "Gina's has the best ice cream," she said, dodging the real question.

He didn't blink. Didn't flinch. Didn't move. He just stood there, still and hard, his gaze fixed on her as his frustration grew. "Why are you back in town?"

She could ask him the same question. Last she knew, he was pre-med at Notre Dame on a full ride football scholarship, following his dreams to get out of this town. But she couldn't ask him, and she couldn't answer him. Telling him she was here to dig up the keepsake box that she and Peyton had buried in her backyard the morning of their graduation, the day Peyton had died, didn't seem like something she should mention.

"Halle," he warned when she didn't say anything, then he took a single step toward her. She wanted to retreat, but she was frozen. The mere sight of him reminded her how easily he consumed her. The way his body had felt wrapped around hers. How he'd worshiped her with his hands and mouth and…oh God.

Finally, her mind sent the signal to her limbs, and she managed to stand and back away. Only, it didn't make a bit of difference. He invaded any semblance of space she created. They were so close now. If she wanted to, she could reach out and touch him.

"Why did you come back?" he asked again.

She was vaguely aware of the handful of people in the diner. He'd always had that blinding effect on her. But she wasn't about to get into this here. That was the last thing she needed.

When she still didn't answer him, a hauntingly deep sound ripped from his throat, and he shouldered past her.

There was only a moment's hesitation as she watched him leave the diner before her courage gave her a swift kick in the butt and she rushed out after him. He was outside by his motorcycle, reaching for his helmet and looking every shade of furious. She knew just how he felt. Even the breeze from the approaching spring storm couldn't do anything to cool her suddenly heated skin.

"Is this how it's going to be? Picking right back up where we left off?" She could understand his anger, but just walking away from her? Hadn't *anything* changed since they'd last seen each other?

"Fuck, Halle." He spun around to face her, and she gasped, the malice in his eyes framed by a deep rooted pain—a pain she'd created—knocking the air from her lungs. "I haven't seen you in ten goddamn years. And the last time I looked at you was when you were standing over my baby sister's casket for fuck's sake. The casket *you* helped put her in."

His words sliced her open. They took her barely mended wound and shredded the scar keeping her together.

"I know," was all she could say.

He shook his head. "You shouldn't have come back here."

Well, she guessed she had her answer then. Apparently, *nothing* had changed. They were still biting out hateful, hurtful words to each other.

But he was right. She should have never come back.

. . .

Cooper's body felt like it was two seconds from exploding.

Fucking hell.

Halle Morgan.

That face, that perfect face that had been haunting him, filling his nightmares, was staring back at him. Even now, he still wanted her. And that only made it worse.

Looking at her was like looking at his past playing out in real time. Memories of a scrawny, freckle-faced kid singing and dancing around his house with his baby sister, sleeping over and listening to that god awful boy band music.

Without realizing it, he rubbed the heel of his palm over his heart. It fucking hurt. Almost every good memory he had of his baby sister included the woman in front of him. He couldn't look at her without seeing Peyton, and he couldn't see Peyton without picturing the image of her broken body lying lifeless in the middle of the road.

Even when he tried to replay the last day he'd spent with Peyton—the morning of her graduation…fuck…the day she'd died—he couldn't, because Halle was a part of that memory, too.

He'd caught Peyton stealing one of his Notre Dame football T-shirts that morning, stuffing it in a tin box. She'd made some sort of pact with Halle about burying things they loved and writing down their dreams for the future. Then in ten years, they would dig it up to see what came true.

That's why Halle was here.

He yanked the helmet off his bike. He had to go—he needed to get away from her.

He could hear the click of her heels rushing toward him. "Cooper, wait."

He spun around, the hurt in her eyes piercing him like daggers. He couldn't stand that look. The one that told him everything he already knew—he'd failed her. Failed his sister. Failed Halle.

"You're back here for that box, aren't you?" he said.

She looked surprised that he knew, but she didn't say anything.

That was answer enough.

He heaved a sigh, dragging his hand through his hair as he tilted his face toward the storm clouds.

"I promised her, Coop," she said, but he refused to look at her. "Do you want it? You can have it if you—"

"No," he said, harsher than he'd intended. But how could she think he'd want to see it? Whatever Peyton had put in that box represented the hope for a future that never even had a chance. They were just memories. Everything was a goddam memory.

He heard her mutter a strangled, "I'm sorry," yet he couldn't bring himself to look at her.

But then he did...

Her full, pink lips quivered as she suppressed the sob raking through her body, and he saw the glossiness of her unshed tears obscuring her green eyes.

Fuck.

She'd been as much a part of his life as his sister had. Now, here she was, standing an arm's breadth away from him, splintering into fragments he couldn't recognize. And it eroded away another goddamn layer of his heart.

Apparently, she could see the walls he'd carefully erected collapsing, because she sucked in a sharp breath. He'd spent the last ten years burying that shit until it was indistinguishable to him and everyone else. It was just easier that way. But mere minutes in her presence and she saw right through him. As if hell wasn't bad enough, she'd opened the window into his personal purgatory.

Her fingers fluttered to her collarbone. "I'm so sorry," she said, shuffling backward.

Time seemingly slowed as he watched her stumble.

He didn't think, just moved. His helmet dropped to the ground, and his boots smacked against the concrete as he reached for her, his arm encircling her waist. Whether or not she needed him didn't matter. Catching her was instinct. Something he thought would've deteriorated by now. Then again, he should've known himself better than that. He'd always been the one to catch her...

Except the time I walked away.

With a groan, he purged the thought from his mind and instead absorbed the sight of her in his arms. She was fucking beautiful. No memory could do her justice. Her copper hair was longer, curls tumbling to her waist. And her soft body, nothing but sexy, womanly curves, had him starving to see what she looked like beneath her dress.

He knew he shouldn't want to pull her body against his just to feel her arms wind around him again. Just like he knew he shouldn't want to breathe her in and taste her lips.

But he did.

And before he could stop himself, he severed the little space between them and pressed his mouth to hers.

There it was, heaven and hell, all in one kiss. Because the second his lips brushed against her sweet, heart-shaped mouth, his entire body came back to life for the first time in ten years.

She was stiff in his arms for only a heartbeat, then she melted against him, and satisfaction thundered through him as her body molded to his.

It'd never been like this. Never before her and not since her. Her lips on his, her deft fingers curling around his neck, her pillowed curves beneath his grip—it was like her body was created for his.

He'd only experienced the perfection of her body for a single night. Surprised didn't quite cover how he'd felt when she'd crept into his room the night before her graduation. And when he'd reached out for her and she smiled, falling into his arms as if she'd done it a thousand times before? *Christ.*

Her taste had ruined him. No woman had ever tasted so good on his tongue. She'd been warm and soft while he'd pressed into her. Untouched and inexperienced, she'd trusted him to take care of her—and he had. Slowly, he'd savored her as she gave herself to him, her breathy moans bathing him while she came undone around him. And it'd been perfect. So sweet...

And now, as his aching cock hardened against her, she softened. As his tongue plunged into the depths of her mouth, she whimpered. And as his hand raked through her hair, she trembled. Still so sweet...

She slipped her hands around to his chest and coiled her fingers in his shirt. "Cooper," she sighed, pulling him closer to her.

His Halle was all grown up. He didn't even know her anymore, and yet, she was clinging to him as if he was the oxygen she needed to breathe.

The realization was like being punched in the stomach with an iron fist. Instantly, his hands dropped to his sides, and he staggered back. The woman in front of him wasn't the same girl who'd snuck into his room, even if she felt every bit as good in his arms as she had ten years ago. Just like he wasn't the same man she'd fallen in love with. And he knew he couldn't be that man for her, not anymore, not after everything that'd happened.

"What—" she started to say, but her mouth clamped closed as he raised his palms.

"This," he bit out between clenched teeth, his hand flailing between them. "This can't happen."

Except his body wanted it to happen—*needed* it to happen. She was right in his reach, swaying from the result of his lips on hers, and he was tempted to pull her back to him.

Hurt flashed over her features but was quickly replaced by the anger that was there minutes ago. "You're right." Her hand flew to her mouth, and she shook her head. "This was wrong… I can't believe you…we can't…"

He didn't let her finish. What was the point? She was only confirming what he'd said, what he knew was true. He climbed on his motorcycle. For both of their sakes, he had to get out of there.

Chapter Two

Halle fumbled her key into the lock on the front door and tried to catch her breath. She'd just seen the one person she'd hoped to avoid. If it wasn't for the fact that she could still feel the imprint of Cooper's kiss on her lips, she would've convinced herself that it didn't happen. And part of her wished it hadn't.

Shaking her head, she attempted to reel in the after-shocks. What was he trying to gain by kissing her, anyway? It was bad enough that she'd started to cry in front of him. Did he really need to see if her body still had the same reaction to his?

There was really no point in wasting her time thinking about Cooper Bale and his mouth on hers, his hands holding her body to his…shit. If only she could just get him out of her mind.

The moment she stepped inside, the smell of dust and dirt assaulted her. She wrinkled her nose and cleared her throat as she made her way through the house.

She'd been in high school when her father passed away and left her this house. Even now, she couldn't find the heart to sell it. As strange as it was, she kept up on everything—the mortgage, the utilities. She even paid a landscaping company to take care of the yard every summer, plus hired a maintenance company to check all the locks every few months or so.

No one understood her need to hang onto this place. What was she supposed to tell them? She didn't understand it herself. She just knew she couldn't let it go.

Just like she couldn't bring herself to pack up all of her father's things. He'd lived in organized clutter his entire life, and all the books and knickknacks thrown throughout the home had comforted her in his absence. Like pieces of him were strung around every room.

It'd always just been her and her dad growing up. Her mom had left when she was a toddler, claiming she was too young to be a wife and mother, rambling a load of crap about how she'd needed to experience life. It didn't matter how she'd wrapped it up and presented it to them. Her mom had abandoned her. Simple as that. The last Halle knew, she was living on the west coast somewhere. She didn't know for sure and, to tell the truth, she didn't care.

Luckily, she'd never wanted for anything growing up, except maybe more time with her dad. He'd been a great dad when he wasn't working all the time, and when he was, Peyton's parents had picked up the slack. Hell, she'd eaten most dinners at their house and had spent so many nights there she had her own bed in Peyton's room. They'd been like family.

Halle stumbled through the chaos of the hallway and pushed open the office door, rubbing her arms as she glanced around. It was like stepping into the past. Some of her favorite childhood memories of her dad had been created in this room. Now, the only thing created in here were cobwebs.

She backed out of the office, sidestepping a stack of hardbacks on the floor, and shut the door behind her. It wouldn't kill her to clean this place up while she was here. Pack up all her dad's books and remove the accumulation of dust on every surface.

Except tackling this place would take days. The thought alone coated her stomach in liquid ice. She didn't want to spend *days* in this town. Wasn't prepared to. She was already on edge, and she didn't know if she could handle the town gossiping over her brief, unwelcomed return. Hell, she'd just come face to face with Cooper. God knew the better part of Glenley had already caught wind of their little spat, not to mention the stunt he'd pulled kissing her.

She resisted the urge to cross her arms like an inconsolable child when the memory of his kiss flurried a longing through her chest. *Days?* She didn't think she could handle *hours.*

Just try to get through today first.

The mental pep talk pushed her down the hall to her old bedroom, but she hesitated at the door. She tried to remember what it'd looked when she'd last been home. Would her pictures from sixth grade summer camp and senior prom still be shrined on her closet door? Memories of her life here, memories of Peyton…

She felt the grief she'd worked so hard to suppress release like air bubbles in deep water—racing to break the surface. She'd come back to dig up a box that held the most treasured pieces of her past—of Peyton's past—not to think about the life she'd left behind. The things in that box meant more than anything in this room could.

A crack of lightning pierced the silence and she startled, her heart slamming against her chest. Then the rain came, pelting the roof in a steady, rhythmic tempo. She glanced out the window at the darkening sky.

How appropriate.

Without another thought, she went to the garage and grabbed the old, metal shovel her dad had used to clear the porch when it snowed. If she was going to do what she'd come here to do, she needed to do it before she talked herself out of it. A promise was a promise, and the sooner she fulfilled it, the sooner she could get out of there.

. . .

Cooper parked his motorcycle in front of the auto garage and stalked inside. It wasn't that he didn't notice how his abrupt entrance alarmed the handful of customers, waiting in the sitting area, he just couldn't find it in him to give a shit at the moment.

Once he reached the back office, he slammed the door closed behind him.

Halle Morgan.

Lighting struck outside his window, loud and furious, but the storm out there had nothing on the one looming inside him.

Out of sight, out of mind.

Bullshit. He'd never been able to completely clear that

woman from his mind. Now she was back, and he could still taste her on his tongue. Could still smell her on his skin. There was no chance of ridding her from his thoughts now.

"Well, aren't you just a ray of sunshine?"

He turned away from the window, and if he'd been able to kill with a glance, he would've been hauled to the county jail and tried for murder. His friend, Abel, was leaning against the doorframe, folding his arms across his chest as he dissected Cooper's current mood.

"Whoa, man," Abel said, stepping inside. "You okay?"

Talk about a loaded question. Okay? No, he wasn't even close.

Christ. He'd spent the last decade alternating between hoping he'd never have to see Halle again and wanting her. Desperately. Just the sight of her sitting at the diner, eating that ice cream, slammed into him like a goddamn freight train. And it fucking tore him apart. It'd undoubtedly do it again. But tell that to his cock, still throbbing from her lingering taste, because he sure as hell wanted her.

Because she's Halle...

He blew out a breath. Was he okay? No. He was far from okay.

"Still trying to figure it out," he managed.

Abel pushed off the doorframe, giving him a look that called *bullshit*. They'd been friends since they were kids, and had been through hell and back together, so it didn't surprise Cooper that Abel could sniff out his mood. Those months after Peyton died, especially after Cooper's piece-of-shit father split, Abel had been there for him—for his mom. But Abel could relate. He'd grown up knowing a thing or two about deadbeat dads and vacant mothers.

"Your mom good?" Abel asked, his face stringing tight with worry.

His mom hadn't been the same since Peyton had died, and after his parents' divorce, she'd been damn near unrecognizable. It was like there was an ominous black hole lingering in front of her, just beckoning her to take that last step. No matter what Cooper tried to do, he couldn't fix it. Nothing could.

"Yeah, man. I mean, shit, today is rough on her—on all of us. But she's doin' okay." He scrubbed his hand over his face, his body falling back against the wall for support. "Halle's back in town."

Abel's brow furrowed. "Halle?" His eyes went wide with realization. "When?"

"Just now."

"Did you talk to her?"

He nodded. "She was at Gina's."

"Shit. Does your mom know?"

If the anger Cooper felt seeing Halle again was any indication how his mother would feel, there wasn't a chance in hell he'd allow that woman near her. She was too fragile.

"No, and she's not going to know."

"Got it." Abel might have been a stubborn son-of-a-bitch, but he knew when to leave something alone. "Come on"—he nodded toward the door—"let's go get a beer."

Chapter Three

Steady drops of water splashed from Halle's sodden hair as she slumped down on the barstool. Outside, the rain continued, drenching the night with its aggressive melody and blending with the noise from all the vulgar, drunken people around her.

One town over, in the sleaziest bar she could find, she figured it was safe to assume no one would recognize her. She wanted to avoid enduring false enthusiastic hugs or listening to bogus revelations of being missed. All she'd be was a juicy conversation filler for the fine folks of Glenley. She might have had a soft spot for the town, but she refused to indulge them.

Besides, they'd have a hay-day with her if they saw her now. Mud smeared her forearms in random clumps, and her dress was leaving a sizable puddle on the dirty floor. She was a mess.

"Something strong?" the older woman behind the bar

asked. Her dark hair, striped gray along the part, hung in tight permed ringlets around her face.

Halle nodded. "Dirty martini."

The woman got to work pouring the clear liquid into a glass. "You wanna talk about it?"

"Nope," she replied, refusing to meet the woman's eyes. It wasn't as though she was trying to be rude. She just didn't want to talk.

But apparently, the woman didn't value privacy. She plopped a few olives into the glass, slid it toward Halle, and then leaned her forearms down on top of the bar. "Take it from me, sweetheart," she began, placing her hand on top of Halle's. "They ain't worth it. Men don't got a lick of sense in the head. Never had and never will, so don't you sit and stew in their stupidity."

Halle looked up and forced a grateful smile. The woman thumped her palm against the bar before she moved on to another customer.

The warmth of the crowded room relieved her chilled skin, and her trembles finally began to subside, but the ache was still there. It hadn't waned since the moment she'd dug the keepsake box from the ground.

She glanced at her purse and, deciding that self-inflicted torture was her wingman for the night, pulled out the small photograph she'd found in the box.

It was an old picture of Peyton in her princess costume and Halle made up as a zombie. They stood on either side of a grinning, fourteen-year-old Cooper. It was the first year she and Peyton were allowed to trick or treat without adult supervision—as long as they stayed with Cooper and his friends.

Normal teenage boys would've protested the company of their ten-year-old sister and her friend, but not Cooper. Even at fourteen, he'd harnessed such admirable qualities. He'd been so protective of them that night, staying close behind them as they'd gone to every house in every neighborhood within walking distance. Despite his friends running ahead, he'd stayed behind, making sure they were safe as they'd collected unhealthy amounts of candy.

She missed that Cooper. The one with a carefree smile — the Cooper who would do anything for her, who would be there for her.

But the man she'd seen today was no longer that Cooper. She didn't know what angered her more, that he was no longer the careful, thoughtful man she'd grown up adoring, or that this new Cooper still had the ability to summon butterflies in her chest.

Before she knew it, she'd emptied her glass, and the bartender was sliding her another. "Thank you," Halle said, the vodka taming her mood a bit.

With a wink, the woman smiled and walked to the other side of the bar.

"Hey."

The deep voice coming from beside her was unfamiliar...and unwelcome. She didn't want to be bothered. She just wanted to find her big girl panties at the bottom of her glass, take a cab home, and fall asleep without having to think about icy blue eyes or strong rough hands.

"Um, you speak?"

She blinked and turned her head, realizing that she hadn't acknowledged her new barstool buddy. "Sorry," she said, not sounding the least bit apologetic. "Hi."

"Ah, she does speak." The man was brawny with long brown hair that fell to his shoulders and a short, trimmed beard that covered his face. He was unexpectedly good looking. All rough, intimidating features and dark, ominously striking eyes inked with flecks of gold. He looked like every woman's secret—or not so secret—dangerous, criminal, fantasy lover.

"Guilty." She smiled.

Offering her his hand, he introduced himself. "Ace."

Yep, and the name to boot.

"Halle."

"Well, Halle, I've got to say, we don't see too many women like you in here."

"I didn't realize this bar stereotyped their patrons." Which was a lie. That was the exact reason she'd come to this bar. The grime on nearly every visible surface, and the smell of cheap sex and stale beer, gave way to their limited and regular customers. But she wasn't complaining. Her dirty martini was perfect, and the seclusion was exactly what she needed.

Ace laughed and nodded his head, most likely deducing her reasons for being there. "What're you drinkin', sweetheart?" he asked, eyeing the small amount of liquid left in her glass and gesturing with his hand for the bartender to return.

Damn, two down already? "Dirty—"

"She's leaving." Strong hands gripped her shoulders from behind, cutting her off mid-sentence.

Although the startling interruption and the abrupt touch didn't seem to shock her, her accelerating heartbeat could have fooled her. Despite the two martinis' obvious ability to cloud her mind, she knew it was him.

Her eyes closed for a brief moment while a slow build of warmth filled the void in her stomach.

No. No, no, no, no.

Allowing her body to involuntarily soften under his touch was just as bad as doing it knowingly. Within a heartbeat, her muscles coiled to steel and her eyes flew open. She cursed the Grey Goose under her breath and swiveled around on the barstool, cutting her glare to Cooper who, not surprisingly, was standing over her.

He was angry, really angry. His nostrils flared with heavy breaths, and his mouth was pressed in a firm line. But that only served to fuel her own anger.

"I'm not leaving," she snapped. "Did you follow me?"

His large hand wrapped around her upper arm, and he lifted her from her seat, his eyes boring his silent demand into hers.

"Dammit, Cooper. Let go of me," she whisper-shouted between clenched teeth.

"Not until you're out that door."

"Hey, Halle." The voice from behind Cooper caught her attention, and she leaned to the side in search of the face that called her name. A tall man in his early thirties came into view. His large sculpted body was decorated with colorful tattoos peering from beneath his T-shirt. His hair was concealed by a tattered baseball hat, and a familiar dimple drilled deep into his left cheek as he grinned at her. She knew him...

"Abel?"

He nodded, his smile almost sad—sorry. "Just go with him, Halle."

If it wasn't for the pleading look on Abel's face, she would have seriously considered ramming the heel of her palm into Cooper's nose if he didn't let go of her.

Instead, she jerked her elbow back, freeing her arm from Cooper's grasp, snatched her purse from the counter, and with narrowed eyes, and a sulking temper to match, she stomped toward the door.

But of course, in true Cooper-the-asshole-fashion, his arm darted out and caught her around her stomach. "Give me your keys."

Those four words shredded her. She felt the sting prick her skin like thousands of tiny daggers sputtered from his mouth. Did he honestly think she would drive after she'd been drinking? After what had happened to Peyton?

"I wasn't going to drive," she barked, fishing her keys out of the bottom of her purse and slamming them against his chest.

His hand caught the cluster of metal before it dropped to the ground. "Abe, can you pay her tab and drive her car to the garage?" he asked, handing Abel the keys and grabbing her elbow.

"Yeah, man. I got this. Get her home."

The weight of everyone's stare closed in on her as she followed Cooper through the bar. What was she, a child? The moment they stepped outside, she once again jerked out of his hold. "God, what the hell is your problem?" The storm had chilled the night air even more than it had when she'd arrived, and her skin erupted in goose bumps.

"My problem is you. Jesus, Halle. What were you thinking coming to a bar like this by yourself? And you wanna tell me how you planned on getting home?"

"Not that you deserve an explanation"—her eyes narrowed—"but I told you, I wasn't going to drive. How dare you think otherwise? And what does it matter to you, anyway?" Before she allowed him the chance to answer, she spun on her heels and started down the side of the road.

It was dark, this side of town vacant aside from the hole-in-the-wall bar she'd just exited. Heavy raindrops pelted her body, and her vision became blurred with the water accumulating on her lashes. She wrapped her arms around her middle as if by some miracle that would settle the dread, or at the very least shield the rain. It failed on both accounts.

The only way any cabs would be driving down this road was if she called the closest taxi company, forty-five minutes away, and paid an insane amount of money for cab fare. Which she'd planned to do if the asshole and his sidekick hadn't barged in.

As she was digging in her purse for her phone, she felt Cooper's arm encircle her waist.

He hauled her back against his chest. "Goddammit," he murmured against her ear, his hot breath cascading seductive warmth throughout her body. And this time when she shivered, it wasn't from the cold. "It. Matters."

"Let me go." The words left her mouth, but she was close to taking them back. Between her body and her heart screaming different demands at her, she didn't know whether to push or pull. And with the feeling of Cooper's body enveloping her, both demands became more of a necessity.

He didn't let her go. Instead, he pulled her along the side of the bar and into the shadows. She opened her mouth to speak but stopped herself. She didn't want to argue anymore. She didn't think she had the strength—she'd experienced firsthand how heartbreaking his words could be.

When her back collided against the brick wall of the building, she gasped. The coarse stone grated the bare skin of her shoulders as she pressed away from Cooper. She had nowhere to go, nowhere to look other than into the daunting blue eyes staring back at her.

The storm continued around them. The sound of the pouring rain connecting with the earth. The roaring roll of thunder mimicked the tension emitting between their bodies. Water was flowing from the long tufts of hair that hung across Cooper's forehead, streaming over his lips and down his chin. Air hissed between her lips as he braced his hands on either side of her head and bowed his body over her, shielding her from the rain's assault.

"I've tried to let you go," he seethed. "I've tried for ten goddamn years to get the image of you out of my head. And I was managing." His hips pressed against her, and she stifled the cry that formed in her throat. She'd tried to let him go, too. Was still trying…

The warmth of his body melted into hers, and she trembled. She was supposed to hate him, not want him.

"I didn't want to see you again."

The feeling was mutual but that didn't lessen the sting. She flattened her palms against his chest and shoved him, only he didn't budge.

"I didn't come back for you," she said, then took a deep breath, trying to steady her voice. "Seeing you was never my intention. And do I need to remind you that *you* pulled *me* out of the bar?" She tried to squirm out of his imprisoning arms with no success. "Just let me go. Let me leave, and you won't have to see me ever again. I'll make sure of it."

"I can't do that."

"Why not?" she shouted as the burn, stinging her eyes, started creeping into her throat.

"I might hate that you're here—hate the grip that chokes me every single time I look at you." Moving his hands to the sides of her neck, he leaned in close. His words were almost lost to the storm as he whispered, "But that's all I want to do. I want to look into your eyes until I can no longer breathe."

• • •

Cooper watched as Halle's body straightened against him, her breaths coming in short, quick pants.

Thick strands of hair stuck to her lips, and he pushed them away, watching as the anger in her eyes thawed beneath his touch. She wrung him raw and rendered him weak. The urge to tip his mouth to hers and clean the drops away with his tongue threatened to overwhelm him.

He groaned, moved his hand to the nape of her neck, and stepped into her. Her body felt warm against his and eased the chill of the cold air. Her hardened nipples brushed against his chest as she arched her back and pressed into him. Damn, she felt so good.

The moment he pushed the bottom of her dress up her hips, his thigh abrading her through her thin satin panties, her eyes closed, and her mouth parted.

His cock strained against the zipper of his jeans. He wanted her so goddamn bad, wanted to bury himself inside her until the only feeling he was aware of was the bite of her nails on his flesh, until the sharp ring of her heady cries pierced his ears.

"Halle," he whispered, only a sliver of air keeping his lips from connecting with hers.

Green eyes appeared beneath her hooded lids, and the sight of her aroused expression gutted him.

He shouldn't be doing this.

He couldn't want this.

He didn't need this.

Goddammit.

His mouth crushed over hers before he talked himself out of it, and her sweet response was almost too perfect. The satisfying whimper that vibrated along his lips had a direct line to his cock, and his hips thrust against her, earning him yet another sweet cry. Thankfully, the shadows of the night and the thick sheets of rain cloaked their bodies, and he lifted her dress higher.

He threaded his fingers into the hair curling at her nape, then tugged gently, eliciting a gasp from Halle's lips. Their mouths thrashed together, desperate for the contact that only the other could supply, crashing and tugging and tasting each other as if the last ten years had deprived them of all pleasure.

And for him, it had. He managed to go through each day as if the past didn't still have a noose around his heart, fooling himself into believing that he didn't miss her—that what he'd felt for her was long gone. But even after all these years, nothing—no one—ever compared.

"You taste even sweeter than I remember," he murmured into her mouth, unable to break away. Her hands left his shirt and slipped through his hair, her nails digging into his scalp, recreating the sensations of his teeth biting into her bottom lip.

He groaned as she shifted her hips, grinding herself

against his thigh. Goddamn, she most definitely wasn't the demure, inexperienced woman he'd had ten years ago.

He reached between her trembling thighs and cupped her pussy, stroking his finger up the center. "I shouldn't do this," he said, his words barely audible through the dense rasp that coaxed from his lips. He dipped a finger inside her through her panties, the fabric absorbing her slick arousal. She rolled against his hand, and he slipped his fingers underneath the hem of her panties and sank one, then two, deep inside her.

A breathy whimper unfurled over her lips, shooting desire straight through him, and whether he should or shouldn't didn't matter. For the first time in ten years, he felt alive.

• • •

Cooper's touch was sending her head first into a spiral of unrelenting pleasure. How many times had she dreamed of feeling his body embrace hers, of his hands caressing her? She'd thought about what it would be like to be in his arms again, to experience his gentleness again. But he wasn't being gentle with her now.

No. He was devouring her.

Rivets of longing burst through her veins, and she suddenly felt enflamed. The tenderness that was once between them, before life had come and splintered their hearts, was long gone. The only emotion bringing them together now was raw, merciless passion, and it was fused with ten years' worth of anger and resentment.

Yet, for some reason, that didn't stop her.

And she wanted more. The anticipation of him inside

her was becoming unbearable the closer and closer she got to the brink of pleasure.

Her hands fumbled at the waist of his jeans, desperate to get them undone so she could feel him in her hands while his mouth scorched a path down the side of her neck.

She shoved his jeans slightly lower on his hips and freed his cock from his boxers. Greedily, she wrapped her fingers around him. His smooth skin glided effortlessly through her hand, the pouring rain slickening his erection as she stroked him root to tip.

Her pace quickened, and she tightened her grip, enjoying every pleasured sound he made. But then a low, libidinous groan reverberated from deep in his throat, and he pulled his cock from her grasp.

He palmed her bottom, his fingers biting into her bare flesh. "Wrap your legs around me," he urged, lifting her up. She complied, her feet slipping from her rain boots as she encircled his hips with her legs. A whimper escaped her. The feeling of his rock-hard erection against her center made her squirm above him.

With Cooper's arms still wrapped around her, he slid his hand between her thighs from behind and pushed her thong to the side. She waited for it, to feel him sink into her and relieve the clenching throb inside her. Her hips rolled above his hold, seeking him out, beckoning him to fill her.

Cooper's mouth fell to her shoulder, and an anguished sigh trembled against her skin. Then, without warning, he plunged his fingers back into her needy sex. The breath was pulled from her lungs as he hit every nerve inside her. But it wasn't enough. She craved his cock sheathed deep inside her, yearned for the ache she'd felt for so long to finally ease.

"I need *you*. Please," she cried, reaching down between their bodies. Her fingers slipped over the thick vein on the underside of his cock, and he sucked in a tight breath.

"Halle." The word was clipped, strained. Maybe even desperate. And if she wasn't mistaken, the desire she heard in his voice mingled with hesitance.

She rolled against him again, trying to sway him, to urge him to give in. His fingers stroked her deep inside while his cock rubbed against her clit. The friction nearly caused her legs to liquefy as pleasure bloomed fast and merciless inside her. With deliberate force, he thrust his hips, his erection rocking against her sex. A moan tickled its way up her throat, and she lost all strength to try to persuade him to do anything other than the blissful magic he was doing to her body at that very moment.

She was clawing at him, her mouth searing wet, hot kisses along every inch of skin she could reach—wildly trying to get more of him, taste more of him, feel more of him. Her body was tightening, her muscles wringing while he continued to deliciously torture her.

"I've tried to let you go," he said. "I've tried like hell to get the image of fucking you—with my fingers, with my tongue"—he looked at her, then hooked his fingers against her G-spot—"with my cock buried deep inside you until…"

She cried out. The combination of his words, the pressure of his body, the feel of his touch—she was so close.

A pained, wry grin formed on his stubbled face as he watched her. "…until you moan."

Allowing the storm to absorb her cries, she threw her head back and shattered, convulsing into thousands of satiated fragments.

A lewd growl met her ears before his lips fastened on her throat, the flat of his tongue lapping up the steady stream of water as he slowed his fingers.

Just as she felt her mind slip away, her body lost to her orgasm and the sensation of Cooper's mouth, a crack of lightning split through the sky and echoed in her chest. There was no denying the electricity between her and Cooper, but she also couldn't deny how dangerous it was. It screamed disaster and heartache, two things she knew for certain she could never experience with him again.

She dropped her head back against the building. "Cooper." Her voice quivered, and he lifted his head, his eyes honing as he peered at her. The raw need that was darkening his irises began to morph into the emotion she was used to feeling when she looked into his eyes.

Regret.

Chapter Four

Only a few inches separated them. So why was it that Halle felt further from Cooper than she ever had? Distance was a part of them. But this felt different. Not like when he'd gone to college, or when Peyton's death had ripped them apart. Not even when she'd been two-hundred miles away in Ohio.

Their gazes were locked, their breaths hurdling together—heartbeats coinciding. Yet, she was alone, detached from the man who mere seconds ago had shattered her resolve and quenched a longing she'd forgotten existed.

Cooper took another small step away from her, only it felt like a mile.

What was she doing? Whatever it was, she wasn't going to accomplish it standing in the rain, mulling over what'd just happened. Trying to compose herself, she adjusted her dress, peeling the sodden material down from her waist, then slipped back into her rain boots.

If only that'd helped. She was a wreck—her body still

trembled from Cooper's touch, her mind an indecipherable heap of confusion. But as he stood in front of her, his breaths still heavy from their kiss, she realized he wasn't the only one feeling the torture of regret—she was, too.

"Let's go." Cooper's voice held the residue of his arousal, deep and husky, and the words caressed her sensitive body before she even realized what he'd said.

"Go?" she asked, looking at him as if he'd just sprouted a second head. He still expected her to go with him?

"I'm not leaving your ass here, Halle. I stopped to make sure you got home, and that's what I'm doing. So let's go."

The thought to argue popped into her head, but what was the point? He would get his way in the end—he always did.

Without a word, she headed toward the road, slogging through the shallow puddles along the way. She fixed her eyes on the ground, careful to keep space between her and Cooper.

"This way," he deadpanned.

He grabbed on to her wrist, and with a gentle tug, she was pressed against his side. Her heart leaped in her chest, shockwaves sizzling along their connected skin. Briefly, she wondered if he felt the same surge as she had, but quickly stowed it away. It didn't matter. Regardless how right his body felt against hers, she knew it was wrong.

As they reached the front of the building, he pulled her across the deserted street, stopping in front of a large, red truck. If trucks had a truck God, this very well might have been the almighty one. She didn't know much about vehicles, nor did she care, but she knew at first glance this was a truck that caused men to salivate. And it was a hell of a lot nicer than the old rusted Ford Cooper used to drive.

Warmth rippled from her heart with a shallow sigh. She'd loved that old truck, and so had Cooper. He'd always picked her and Peyton up from middle school in that old truck, and when the weather had been warm, he'd taken the back roads and let them sit in the bed so they could make shapes out of the clouds above them.

She smiled to herself. That old Ford held a lot of good memories of her and Peyton. The last time she'd seen that truck was...

She paused, rotating her head to the side to peer at Cooper as the arduous memory came back to her. She hadn't seen that truck since the day he'd peeled out of the cemetery—the moment her already broken world had crumbled.

It was fitting that old truck was gone, because so was the old Cooper.

Halle's gaze refocused when he opened the driver's side door and stepped to the side. "Get in."

She grabbed on to the handle and stepped onto the running board. "Gosh, you need a ladder for this thing," she said, hoisting herself up.

Cooper's hands latched onto her waist, and he lifted her up as she maneuvered into the cab. "You never were very coordinated."

She bristled at his words. His gestures were so much like the old Cooper that for a moment, her heart ached. She glanced back at him, surprised to see a slight smile turning up his lips. But it didn't last long.

"Slide over," he said.

She scooted across the seat, her thighs slicking along the leather. God, his scent consumed her. It was all around her—in the truck, on her skin. The lingering alcohol in her system, combined with his intoxicating scent, made her feel tipsy all over again.

Without looking at her, Copper climbed in the truck and shut the door behind him. The overhead light dimmed, leaving only the moon and the lightning to aid her eyes as she watched him peel off his shirt. She swallowed. The moonlight soaked the contours of his abs in a cool glow, while bolts of lightning flashed like a spotlight on his chest. She couldn't stop from staring.

He balled up his shirt and tossed it in the backseat. "Take your dress off," he said, reaching behind him.

She blinked. "Excuse me?"

He straightened back around and tossed her a crumpled up T-shirt. "It's not clean, but it's dry," he said, starting the truck.

She stared at the shirt in her hands. It was light gray, smudged with auto grease and smattered with dirt. But that wasn't what stalled her. To be wrapped in his shirt—covered in nothing but his scent—she feared she'd lose control. Her body was rebelling against her heart, winning the war of confliction in her mind. She couldn't risk it.

"Take off your dress," Cooper demanded, his eyes searching her face as she peered at him.

"I'm fine." She set his shirt down on the seat between them.

"Like hell you are. You're soaked. Get out of that dress and put my shirt on."

A little chivalry was one thing, but his unwarranted concern was beginning to give her whiplash. "Just drive. I'm fi—"

"Goddammit, Halle. I'm not arguing with you." He picked the shirt up off the seat and tossed it in her lap. "Put the damn shirt on. I'm not leaving here until you do."

Of course he wasn't—he was just as stubborn as always. With a frustrated sigh, she arched her back, lifting her bottom from the seat so she could pull her dress up over her hips. She immediately felt Cooper's eyes on her, unashamed as he watched her every move.

Her nipples tightened beneath her bra as she lifted her dress over her head and dropped it to the floorboard. A low hiss sliced through the cab of the truck. Sure, Cooper had just pinned her to a building and made her come so hard she could still feel the aftershocks. But the desire she saw pooling in his gaze, laboring his breaths as she sat nearly naked beside him, reached a new level of vulnerability.

With no remorse, his eyes ravaged her, appreciating her body with long, penetrating sweeps. Goose bumps scattered across her body, and she held her breath. She was embarrassed and turned on all at once, unable to move a muscle under the weight of his stare.

Absentmindedly, she brushed her thighs together, and her breaths started coming in short pants. She itched to reach out and touch him, to skim her nails down his bare chest—to feel his muscles tremble beneath her fingertips. But she didn't move.

He looked at her without apology. And she did the same. Water rolled down his chest as if it were a maze, dripping around and over each hard muscle. A blaze of heat flamed inside her, intense and raw, and without even realizing it, she'd inched toward him. As though his gaze alone had pulled her.

Cooper shifted in his seat, the muscles of his thighs bunching, drawing her attention to his hard erection. His jeans were soaked, and the denim clung to his cock. She easily saw the thick head, ridged perfectly above his massive length.

When she looked up at him, his eyes were hard, ringed with constrained lust as he watched her look at him. She licked her lips, a small moan slipping out of her.

"Fuck," Cooper muttered, recoiling back into the seat. He closed his eyes briefly, running his hand over his face and through his dripping hair as a tortured sigh heaved from his chest. "Put the damn shirt on."

She picked up the shirt, scrambling to pull it over her head. And just as she suspected, it smelled like him. Like sandalwood and rain, covered with a faint scent of automotive oil. Not to mention the worn fabric felt heavenly.

More silence pivoted around them as he pulled onto the road and drove through the desolate town. The rain continued to beat down from the sky, beating a cathartic, steady rhythm on the truck. In the quiet like this, she could almost pretend the undeniable hell forged between them was no longer there. As if this night was like any other night that could have been. But the hard reality was, it wasn't.

Rolling her head back onto the seat, she asked, "How did you know where I was? Did you follow me?"

"No," he stated, quickly cutting his eyes to hers before returning them to the road. "I didn't follow you. Abe and I were driving past and saw your car."

"What were you doing in Fayette?" The town was just a couple of miles from Glenley, but it was half Glenley's size—and that wasn't saying much. Besides a couple of hole-in-the-wall bars, the quick-stop gas station, and the diner, there wasn't much else to it.

"You're not the only one who'd rather drink away their living hell in peace," he muttered.

Drink away his living hell? He'd gone to ease his misery at the bottom of a bottle just like she had. And his misery was her...

That should have saddened her, or maybe even infuriated her, but at this point, she'd expected it. Could she blame him if seeing her after ten years warranted a little alcohol infused distraction? Seeing *him* sure as hell did.

He didn't say another word after that, just continued to fix his attention to the dashing lines on the road. And she couldn't help but fix her attention on him. Even with the looming darkness that hovered around them, lust still saturated the air and clung to her like heavy dew. She couldn't escape it.

But she couldn't take the silence. It crawled beneath her skin—almost painful. Yet, she didn't know what to say, and Cooper didn't seem to care enough to fill the quiet, either.

Several minutes later, Copper pulled onto her road. She clutched her chest and looked at him. It wasn't fair, wanting something she couldn't have while hating it in equal measure.

"Abel and I will drop your car off before morning," he said, glancing at her.

There was her marginal opportunity to try and ease some of the tension. Or at the very least pretend. "So you two are still friends? I almost didn't recognize—"

"Halle," Cooper interrupted. His voice was level, but authority boomed through the cab of the truck, sending chills across her arms. "We're not doing this. I can't do the small talk, okay?"

She nodded, shifting her head to look out the window as

Cooper turned down her driveway. "Okay." She didn't know why she even tried. It wasn't as though any of their conversations in the last few hours, scratch that, the last decade, had been civil.

When he rolled the truck to a stop, she faced him and waited for him to say something, to acknowledge her, but he remained focused on the moving wiper blades in front of him.

"Why'd you do it?" she blurted out, her voice nearly shouting as she allowed her frustration to ferment into anger. "Why'd you kiss me if you can't even look at me?"

Only he didn't answer. Didn't even look at her.

"Why did you pretend you cared, Coop?" It was as if her words finally penetrated the barrier between them, and he turned and faced her—only she wished he hadn't. The look in his eyes would haunt her forever—pain, regret…and longing.

"Go," he bit out between clenched teeth.

Breath lurching from her chest, she tore out of the car. The man was confusing and completely impossible. And he'd just solidified the fact that she didn't belong here anymore. Tomorrow, she would go back to Ohio, back to her life away from this small town that had nothing left for her—nothing but memories.

• • •

"You good, man?" Abel asked as he shut the door to Halle's car and started toward Cooper's truck. "You wanna go check on her?"

Cooper pulled his gaze away from Halle's house. The

porch light was on, but the rest of the lights were off—meaning she was probably already asleep. And just the thought of her curled up in bed made him want to storm through the front door and cover her body with his.

"Coop, dude?"

Blinking, Cooper shifted his attention to Abel. "No," he finally replied. "I don't want to check on her. She'll be fine. She's probably passed out." Which was a lie. He was using every shard of strength he had to keep from checking in on her.

"All right," he said, sighing.

"What?"

Abel opened the passenger-side door. "Nothing."

"That's bullshit. You got something to say, then say it," he said, glaring at Abel over the hood of his truck.

"It's Halle, man. Little Halle. The same girl who used to dig up worms for you so you'd let her tag along with us when we went fishing. The same girl who camped out on your bedroom floor with Peyton after we dared them to watch *Poltergeist*. The girl who cried on your shoulder when her dad died. Fuck, man. She's the same girl you—"

"She's not that girl anymore." Cooper jerked his door open and threw himself in the truck. He didn't need a reminder of how every single part of his life up till ten years ago included her. He didn't need a reminder, because the very moment he'd seen her again, all those memories had come rushing back. But they weren't the people they used to be. How could he be after he'd let Peyton down, after he'd turned his back on Halle, after he'd let his mom slip through his fingers?

It was simple. He couldn't.

Abel climbed in the truck. "Yeah, well, she's fucked you up something good in the short time she's been back in town."

Cooper cut his eyes to him.

Abel laughed. "See? You look like you're about to take a swing at me right now."

He flexed his fingers and rolled his head from side to side. Years of anger and guilt combined with the ache in his balls twitched beneath his skin. He was restless and agitated, and Abel was taking the brunt of it.

Shifting the truck into reverse, Cooper glanced at the house one last time before turning to look out the rear window. "Let's just go."

After dropping Abel off at the garage, Cooper made the routine drive down his childhood road. He didn't usually stop by his mom's house this late. It was well after midnight. But after seeing Halle—after all the shit that resurfaced from looking into her goddamn eyes—he knew he wouldn't be able to go home until he checked on his mom.

Quietly, he opened the door, kicked his muddy boots off, and stepped inside. The familiar smell of his childhood no longer filled this house. It was stale and infused with gloom.

He could hear the faint voices coming from the T.V. in the living room as he walked down the hall. His mother always had the TV on, if for nothing but the noise to fill the permanent silence that roared throughout the house. What was once a home of laughter and happiness was now his mother's prison.

And there she was, sitting in the recliner asleep. The

ever present pang in his chest tightened as he looked at her frail body curled in on itself, a bottle of anti-depressants and sleeping pills on the end table along with an empty glass of wine.

It was nothing unusual. The wine. The anti-depressants. But the sleeping pills only came out once a year—on the anniversary of Peyton's death.

She was just a shell of the mother he once knew. The vibrant woman who loved and laughed, baked cookies, and decorated for the Fourth of July was gone. She was empty now.

Maybe if he'd stayed around the weeks after Peyton's death instead of trying to lose his grief out on the road, then maybe he could've prevented all this. But he'd bailed, trusted his dad to take care of the only woman he had left in his life.

Turned out the apple didn't fall far from the fucking tree, because Cooper's dad split a few months later. His dad had been grieving, and seeing his wife wither into a woman he didn't recognize had been too much for him. Part of Cooper felt sorry for the bastard—losing his daughter, and essentially, his wife. But his dad should have stayed and taken care of her. Instead, he'd bowed out like a fucking coward, and if Cooper never saw him again, it would be too soon.

Cooper hadn't hesitated dropping out of Notre Dame the beginning of his senior year to move home and take care of his mom. He'd owed her that much—hell, he owed her a lot more.

Looking at the untouched plate of spaghetti and meatballs on the kitchen table, he sighed, picked up the plate, and put it in the sink. It was like this most nights. He came to his mom's house and cooked her dinner every evening, and more often than not her food went untouched. She subsisted on cereal and tea, and the occasional cup of Jell-O or pudding if he was lucky.

After walking into the living room and shutting off the TV, he gathered his sleeping mother in his arms. She was weightless as he carried her down the back hall. Bones protruded through her thin, pale skin, her blond hair tied away from her sallow face.

She shifted in his arms, her muscles tensing. "Cooper," she mumbled, her eyes fluttering beneath her lids as she struggled to return to consciousness.

"Yeah, I got you, Mom. Go back to sleep."

"Thank you," she whispered, her body once again relaxing in his hold as he carried her into her room.

He lay her down in bed and pulled the covers up, untangling them from their disheveled heap at the foot of the mattress before tucking her in. He leaned down and pressed a kiss to her forehead. "Night, Mom. I'll see you tomorrow."

"Hmm." She was already drifting back asleep.

He shut the door behind him and walked back down the hall, but he paused—stopping in front of Peyton's room—something he'd never done. He'd walked past her bedroom thousands of times over the years, but never once had he allowed himself to take a moment to stop at her door. Never once had he gone inside. He couldn't bear to go in there and see his baby sister's life frozen in time.

So why now, after all these years, did he have the urge to barge through the goddamn door?

He dropped his forehead to the door and slammed his fist against the wood, thick splinters falling at his feet.

He knew the answer.

Halle.

She'd be in that room, too. Her things would still loiter the space alongside his sister's. Memories of the Halle who'd basically grown up in this house would be embedded in everything he saw.

Her very presence shifted the ground beneath his feet. He'd thought he was done with the past. With her. But the past wasn't done with him, and neither was she. He reached for the comforting numbness he'd grown attached to, but instead, found the memory of how her soft, wet body felt clinging to him. And God help him, he wanted to feel her again.

Chapter Five

It was only a dull throb, but the uncomfortable tapping inside Halle's head jostled her from sleep. Groaning, she peeled her cheek from the leather couch, rolled to her back, and stretched out her legs. It would have been much more comfortable had she slept in her bed, but after her night with Cooper, all she'd wanted to do was crash and escape her thoughts. And changing the sheets to the fresh ones she'd brought from home would have required *way* too much effort.

She sat up and lowered her legs to the floor. Her neck was stiff, and her head swam as blood rushed through her body. Focusing her eyes, her gaze landed on the muddy plastic bag resting beneath the tin box that was sitting on the coffee table where she'd left it last night.

"Uhh," she moaned, dropping her head to her hands to rub her temples. If seeing that old Halloween picture had sent her on a vodka-induced mission, she wasn't sure she could withstand the reaction she would have if she looked at everything else in that box.

Only, that was the entire reason she came back to this town. She'd promised Peyton no matter where she was or what she was doing, they would meet back at this house and dig up their memories.

It took all her strength, but she finally leaned forward and popped off the lid. Stalling wouldn't change the fact that she had a promise to fulfill. And the sooner she fulfilled it, the sooner she could get out of town. Then maybe she had a fighting chance of moving on.

Yeah, right. She had a better chance of snagging Gina's homemade ice cream recipe. She couldn't possibly move on now that she'd collided head first with Cooper. Now that she'd felt his mouth on hers. Seen a glimpse of the Cooper she'd yearned for ever since she'd left.

Damn him.

Why did he have to kiss her? The look in his eyes alone rendered her body his hostage, but his touch? It was as if every good memory was forged from his fingertips. And she'd been powerless to stop it.

Because it was *Cooper.*

Shivers tickled her flesh as phantom sensations of his expert touch accompanied her thoughts. He was everything she'd ever wanted. Now the only thing she wanted was to get far away from him. Preferably sooner rather than later.

She reached into the box and shuffled through some more photos, careful to keep her eyes from examining them too long.

She couldn't do this. Shaking her head, she grabbed the lid, but a pink bead sticking out beneath one of the photos captured her attention.

It was her and Peyton's old friendship bracelets. Peyton's mom, Kathryn, had taken them to the mall when they were twelve, and they'd seen the cheesy bracelets in one of those cheap jewelry stores. A warm ache spread though her at the memory. The words "Best Friends" were engraved on a silver heart charm that was split down the middle—each bracelet holding half. She and Peyton had been so proud of their bracelets, even promised to never take them off.

She smiled. Promises were easily broken, but not when it came to theirs. They'd worn those damn things every single day. Even in high school, when the childish jewelry was a hindrance to their impending fashion statements, or lack thereof, they'd still worn them.

To this day, their promises weren't easily broken—it was why she was here.

After clasping her bracelet around her wrist, she studied its matching half in the palm of her hand. Peyton would want her mom to have this.

God, but things ended so horribly all those years ago. She and Cooper had a fight after Peyton's funeral, and she'd left the next day without much of an explanation to anyone—including Peyton's parents—and they'd deserved better than that after everything they'd done for her. Especially Kathryn.

Unease rolled through her stomach. Just the idea of facing Peyton's parents after all this time made her palms sweat and her heart squeeze. But if she didn't go to them now, she never would.

Except, what if Cooper was there? There was no way she could face him after last night. She'd gotten out of his truck with as much of her dignity intact as possible after practically mauling him outside the bar. Seeing him again would only dissolve what little was left.

So why did excitement flutter in her chest at the very thought? She groaned and threw herself back against the couch. He was a double-edged sword—and she'd been cut one too many times.

She looked at the bracelet in her hands.

Get it together.

This was her last day here—her last chance to see Kathryn. If she saw Cooper's truck or motorcycle, she'd just keep on driving. But she at least had to try. Hopefully, seeing Kathryn would go better than seeing Cooper.

The rain had stopped, but the ground was sodden and the air was damp. Halle sat there and stared at Peyton's house, her other childhood home, and chewed on her lip. She straightened her shirt, her fingers fumbling over the hem. She knew coming to this house would be hard; she just hadn't realized how hard. It was only a house. Just walls. But it terrified her. What if Kathryn didn't want to see her?

Things had been different between her and Kathryn after the accident. Kathryn had stayed in the hospital with Halle while Mr. Bale and Cooper had taken care of Peyton's funeral arrangements. Yet, she hadn't really been *there*. She'd helped the nurses take care of her—changed the bandages on her cuts, helped her do the little things her broken arm prevented her from doing—but Kathryn hadn't spoken to her.

Guilt hung from Halle's shoulders like a blanket of ice. Halle was alive, and Peyton was dead. Of course Kathryn hadn't spoken to her. Halle hadn't sought out her conversation, either. Not that it would've mattered. No words could have soothed Kathryn's pain.

Come on, Halle. Pull yourself together. You can do this.

With no sign of Cooper anywhere, she turned the car off and stepped out. She exhaled, both relief and disappointment unfurling from her lungs. Though she didn't feel up to entertaining the reasons why.

The house looked so different. What used to be a beautifully landscaped yard, spattered with dozens upon dozens of colorful flowers, was now bare, apart from the mulch and shrubs. The shades were all drawn, and the front porch, where her favorite swing had once been, was now nothing more than a concrete slab.

With a deep breath, she rapped on the door, and then felt her heart stop as the knob began to turn. Yes. This was definitely a mistake. What did she expect? A warm welcome and a tight embrace from the woman who was practically her mother growing up, a woman she hadn't seen or spoken to in ten years?

No, she couldn't do this. If Kathryn looked at her the same way Cooper had, she didn't think she could bear it.

But even though she desperately begged her limbs to retreat, she didn't budge.

When the door finally opened, a woman she didn't recognize stood slumped in the doorway. Instantly, guilt churned Halle's stomach, and she thought she was going to be sick.

This woman wasn't Kathryn. It had to be a dream— a nightmare—because this *couldn't* be real. Dark circles haunted her features, as if all the life was sucked from her beautiful face. Her body was so very thin, and her blond hair was streaked heavily with gray. She looked tired, defeated.

Kathryn stared at her for what seemed like a lifetime before her eyes widened. Every muscle in Halle's body was strung tight, her heart crushing her lungs.

"Halle?" Kathryn asked, her soft voice cracking as if she hadn't spoken in a long time.

She forced herself to smile. "Hi, Kathryn."

Blinking, Kathryn moved to the side. "Come in."

Sorrow collided with her the moment she stepped inside. It hung in the air, lingering like a rain cloud after a heavy storm. The house was dim and quiet—nothing like she remembered.

After following Kathryn into the kitchen, Halle sat down at the table across from her.

"You're all grown up." Kathryn's voice, her words, they were almost robotic, all the warmth gone. She never imaged this, never in a million years.

She shifted her gaze to her hands. "Yeah."

Halle could feel Kathryn's stare penetrating her, so she looked up, and it was as if she could see a memory pass through her eyes.

Kathryn's mouth quivered. "It seems like just yesterday you…"

Reaching across the table, she snatched Kathryn's hand and gave it a tender squeeze. They didn't need to do this. Not now. As badly as Halle wanted to unload the pile of questions accumulating in her mind, she didn't.

"I know." She stood up, walked around the table, and stopped next to Kathryn's chair. Without another thought, her arms darted out and wrapped around Kathryn's shoulders. Her small frame felt fragile beneath Halle's embrace. God, it was heartbreaking. And it was all her fault.

If ever there was a moment she had to be strong, it was now. She placed the bracelet on the table, then walked to the stove. Her hands braced on the counter for just a moment while she took in a deep breath, then she sprang into action. Just like she'd done a hundred times before, she filled the tea kettle with water, then bagged the loose leaf, orange blossom tea—exactly the way Kathryn liked it.

"Thank you, Halle."

Her fingers stumbled, and the tea bag dropped to the counter. She felt the air in her lungs freeze, her guilt and pain burning her like liquid ice when she heard Kathryn speak again. "I'm so glad you're home."

. . .

What a miserable day.

Since Cooper had been a boy, tinkering around on trucks and cars with his dad before he was even old enough to read, restoring old vehicles had been his private escape. His garage closed up early on Saturdays, and for the last four hours, he'd been elbows deep under the hood of his old 1970s Ford 100 pickup. But not even the beauty of a brand new engine and the smell of oil could distract his mind from recalling the way Halle's curves twisted and moved as she'd stripped her wet dress from her slick body. Or the way her perfume had clung to his skin. Not to mention the way every sweet sound she'd made as he drove her to orgasm seemed to be on repeat in his mind.

Even now, with the windows down and the wind tunneling through his truck, he could still smell her. Rain mixed with perfume.

So yeah, it was a miserable day spent trying, and failing, to rid the one woman he didn't want to think about from his thoughts. All it did was grant him a case of blue balls and ensured his frustration.

Once he pulled into his mom's driveway, he killed the engine and grabbed the grocery bags from the seat. He'd told Abel to stop by for dinner. Figured he'd throw a couple steaks on the grill. Even though his mom never really said much to either of them, he knew she liked having them there.

Trying not the drop the groceries, he maneuvered the bags in his arms, unlocked the door, and then shoved it open with his shoulder. "Hey, Mom," he hollered out as he kicked the door shut and started toward the kitchen.

His mouth began to salivate as the aroma of baking meatloaf wafted through the air around him, his stomach immediately rumbling in approval. Damn that smelled delicious.

Wait a minute.

He, and occasionally Abel, were the only people who ever cooked in this house anymore, and neither of them ever made a meal that smelled as good as the one cooking right now.

"Mom?"

When he reached the kitchen, he almost dropped the bags to the floor. He didn't know whether to laugh or fucking cry as he gaped at his mom standing over the stove, poking at a pot of boiling potatoes. He couldn't even remember the last time she did anything other than lay on the couch or sit in her chair. She would barely eat, let alone cook anything.

The table wobbled as he dumped the bags on top of it. In a few short strides, he crossed the kitchen and then wrapped his arms around her, kissing the back of her head. It felt like he'd waited a lifetime to see her like this again. "Smells good, Mom."

When she looked up at him over her shoulder and smiled, he swore his heart stalled. It wasn't a full smile, but he saw a glimpse of his mother in that smile—the one he was beginning to forget. And it damn near sent him to his knees.

"Would you mind setting the table?"

Still shocked, he tried to wrap his head around the scene playing out before him. He wanted to question the change in her, figure out what in the hell had cleared some of the fog she'd been living in for the last ten years. But he didn't want to risk losing this—risk shifting her back into the void she'd escaped in to.

"Yeah, sure," he finally replied, grabbing plates from the cabinet.

"Abel coming for dinner tonight?"

Goddamn.

She almost sounded like her old self. There was a lightness to her voice, a slither of happiness had somehow absorbed into her. It was almost like he was a teenager again. It felt like all the times she would insist Abel come eat a real home cooked meal with them.

"Actually, yeah. He should be here anytime."

"Good," she said, her smile extending a little more this time.

He returned a sappy-ass grin—he couldn't help it. He loved seeing her like this. But the moment his eyes honed on the table, his mouth went slack, and he lost the ability to breathe. The colorful piece of jewelry his sister had worn every damn day was sitting on the table as if she'd just taken it off and left it there.

The clank of the ceramic plates hitting the table jarred him from his stupor. Instantly, questions scrambled through his thoughts. But they were pointless, because he knew every goddamn answer.

It was Halle.

He should've known this little piece of happiness came with a price.

Halle had been here. She'd brought his mom the bracelet, and he knew she was the reason for her sudden transformation.

"Mom, I need to run somewhere really quick, but I'll be back before dinner is ready. And Abe will be here soon, so let him know if you need any help." He scooped the bracelet from the table, his grip indenting the small beads into his palm.

His mom simply nodded, offering a fraction of a smile, but a smile nonetheless.

As he stalked out the door, he almost trampled Abel as they collided on the porch.

"Fuck, man. What's wrong?"

He spared a glance at Abel, then heaved out a cluster-fuck of emotions in one long sigh. "Mom's cooking."

Abel's brows gathered. "She's what?"

Yeah, that's what he'd thought to. "I'll be back. Help her out, will ya?"

"Sure, of course."

Confusion creased Abel's face, but Cooper didn't have the time to explain. He shouldered past Abel and jogged down the driveway.

"Coop?"

The door bounced back as he threw it open, pausing just long enough to look over the hood at Abel.

"Halle?"

Jaw tightening, teeth clenched, he nodded. "Yeah. Halle."

The engine roared as he started the truck, the bracelet still firmly in his grip. He couldn't decide if he was pissed that she'd come to his mom's house, or pissed that after all this time, she was the one to yank his mom from the hell she'd been barely surviving in. Either way, he was going to talk to her.

Chapter Six

It didn't take Halle long to get together the few things she'd brought with her. Last night was proof enough of the damage staying in this town could cause, and after seeing Kathryn, seeing another person's life ruined because of her stupid mistake, she couldn't endure staying here any longer.

She was double-checking the lock on the back bay window, when a loud, insistent knock thundered on the front door.

"Shit," she muttered, catching her finger in the window's latch.

Now that her heart was lodged in her throat, she whipped around and stared down the narrow hall to the entry. Another round of pounding commenced. She knew without a doubt Cooper was standing on the other side of that door, and the very knowledge sped her pulse and aggravated a swarm of salacious butterflies in her stomach.

She sucked the cut on her finger and debated ignoring

him, of just sinking down on the sofa and waiting until he gave up and left. Except that thought ricocheted a longing through her chest until the very threads holding her heart together threatened to snap.

She hadn't wanted to see him, hell, after his blunt dismissal last night, she was determined to never see him again. But now that he was here, she *needed* to see him—one last time—if only to say goodbye.

Seriously, Halle?

It was stupid; it would probably destroy her. Actually, she knew it would. But he was here. This was her chance to prevent history from repeating itself—her chance to leave without tears in her eyes.

Taking a breath, she hurried down the hall and threw open the door before she was able to talk herself out of it. And although she was prepared to see him staring back at her, it didn't prevent her heart from plummeting to the pit of her stomach from the sight of him.

He met her eyes and dropped his hand from where it hovered in the air from banging on the door. His breaths were short and fast, as if he'd sprinted here. Oil covered his white T-shirt, and his faded jeans were worn thin, clinging to his thighs and hanging tattered over his work boots. Wavy sandy-brown tufts of hair stuck out from beneath his baseball hat, shadowing the emotions swirling in his gaze. But she could deduce what they were.

Anger. Desire.

She felt them, too.

"Yes?" she blurted when she was finally able to find her voice around the need crawling up her throat.

He didn't answer at first, just rolled his shoulders with

an exasperated sigh. "We need to talk." His words were a guttural sound deep in his throat.

Then he extended his hand and opened his fingers — and she saw the bracelet.

Shit.

She stepped outside and shut the door. Instantly, he towered over her. With every labored breath, his muscles tightened, his sculpted body so close she could feel the warmth from his chest.

Blood quickened through her veins as she lifted her chin to look at him. He wasn't just angry, he was furious. Yet, when his stare drifted to her lips, his eyes darkened with need. Her heart couldn't handle his temper *and* his touch, not again.

"I'm listening, so talk."

He raised his eyes back to hers. "You want to explain why the hell you thought it was a good idea to visit my mom?"

Her brows knitted together, and she latched her hands onto her hips. "Because I thought she would like to have the bracelet. Is that so wrong?"

"Yes. You have no idea… You can't… She could have…"

He laced his hands atop his head and spun around, tipping his face to the sky as he stomped toward the porch steps. "For the last ten years, I've been taking care of her, trying to bring her back," he shouted into the night. He spun around again and was back in front of her with two long strides. "I'm failing miserably, but I'm *trying*."

She examined the shallow creases that lined his eyes, the pain that bowed through his expression. She bit her lip and floated her fingers across his cheek. No matter how mad she was, she couldn't stand to see him suffering. Because underneath it all, he was still Cooper.

He yanked her hand from his face, and she gasped. "What if seeing you had broken her even more? What if looking at you after all these years had gutted her, just like it did me? Then what?"

"Is that what you think I wanted? To hurt you? To hurt Kathryn?" she shouted, her anger infusing her with courage. "I would never!"

He laughed, the sound anything but light. "Funny, because you didn't seem to care about hurting anyone when you decided to let that drunk idiot drive you home."

Halle folded her arms across her chest, as if she could shield herself from his verbal lashing. His words, they were his weapon of choice, and they always defeated her. She couldn't let that happen again.

"Nice, Cooper. That's not fair, and you know it."

"Not fair? What's not fair is that my baby sister is dead. *Dead*. You might have been Peyton's best friend, but my mother loved you like her own daughter, and you hightailed it out of here before the dirt even covered Peyton's casket."

"You're right, I did. But what was I supposed to do? I was eighteen. I had nothing left here, Cooper. My dad was dead, my best friend was dead, and I'd just destroyed the lives of the only other family I had." She dropped her gaze, focusing on the wooden boards beneath her feet. "I was scared. And after our fight at the cemetery, you made it pretty clear you never wanted to see me again."

She remembered that day almost as clearly as the day she'd first given her body to him. Ironic, considering one submersed her with love, the other tore her open with hate.

They'd been standing beneath the large Sycamore at the

edge of the cemetery right after Peyton's service. It was the first time he'd spoken to her since the accident.

She could hear his words as if he was saying them all over again.

"Peyton never would've gotten in a car with a drunk driver. But she was following you. All because…." He gritted his teeth and shook his head.

"Cooper, don't go. Don't leave me," she said as he tore the truck door open and threw himself inside.

"I can't be near you, Halle. I can't look at you right now."

She swallowed hard as the memory settled back in her mind. She knew his words were born from his heartache, but he'd only speared her with the truth. How could he have thought she'd stick around after that? Her heart had been broken, and he'd left her.

She could feel tears swelling behind her eyes, but she refused to release them. She wouldn't give him the satisfaction of seeing her pain. "It's getting late. What do you want with me, Cooper?"

His stance widened. "It doesn't matter what I want."

"Then why are you here?"

"Because for the last ten years, my mom has been nothing but a shell. She hardly ever leaves the house, she barely speaks to anyone, she doesn't eat, and the only time she gets any sleep is when she's popped an anti-depressant and washed it down with wine." He took off his baseball hat and ran a hand through his messy hair before shoving it back on. She watched as the words turned over in his mouth, but no sound left his lips.

"But today, when I got to her house to cook her dinner, you know what I saw?" he asked as he shoved his hands in his pockets.

Halle pressed her lips together. She didn't want to know. What if something had happened after she'd left? What if Cooper was right?

Shaking her head, she squeezed her eyes shut, but he wouldn't allow it. He grasped her chin, his deep timbre vibrating her skin. "She was smiling."

She blinked up at him. "What?"

"I don't know what you said to her—"

"I didn't say anything, I just—"

"—but you got through to her somehow. You brought back a piece of the woman I used to know. And I haven't seen her in a long damn time."

The way his voice softened when he spoke of his mother made her remember an eighteen-year-old Cooper giving his mom his football jersey to wear to the game on senior night. He could never be accused of not loving his family. She'd never known a man who adored the women in his life more than Cooper. He would do anything for his mom, just like he would have done anything for Peyton. Even for her.

A tear escaped and he caught the single drop with his thumb while his gaze focused on her lips.

And she shivered.

His touch had become tender. But his eyes, they remained cold, frozen like a glacier of ice in the deepest, bluest part of the ocean. Beautiful and dangerous.

Her lids drifted closed for a moment, and she sucked in a breath. "Just tell me what you want."

Her heart whispered a plea that he would say he wanted her. That he longed for her touch the same way every inch of her body seemed to long for his at that very moment—when his walls were slightly lowered, and she could see pieces of the man she once loved.

"I want you to spend time with her."

She jerked her head from his grasp. "What? No," she insisted. That was that last thing she ever imagined he would ask her.

"This isn't easy for me, either," he said gently, the considerate lilt to his voice taking her by surprise. "You think I want to see you in the house I grew up in again like nothing ever happened? You're the last person I'd want to help my mom, but as it turns out, you're the only one who can."

Her scalp prickled, and her stomach quivered as unease settled in her chest. It was hard enough seeing Kathryn, there was no way she could go back. And being around Cooper...

It was too hard.

Still, she couldn't deny the twinge of hope that sparked. There were countless nights she'd dreamed he'd come for her, asking her to stay with him just like he was now. But this wasn't a dream. He didn't want her—he needed her help. And she'd seen how being around her affected him. She'd rather leave town than see him hurt again.

"I can't."

"Bullshit," he barked. And there he was, back in new and improved Cooper fashion. His movements were sleek and quick as he stepped into her. His body ran along hers, pressing her back against the door as he loomed over her. "You can. And you will." Placing his hands on the door on either side of her head, he angled his mouth to her ear and whispered, "You owe her that much."

His lips fluttered over her earlobe, and her hands flew to his biceps. She felt herself softening into him as he pressed against her. Her breaths became jagged, but she remained motionless.

A harrowing groan escaped Cooper's throat. He might not be the same man she'd known all her life, but she *knew* him. His pain was as palpable as her own—and so was his desire.

"So what, you want me to stay here? In Glenley? You know how bad the gossip will get once people find out I'm back."

Leaning into her even more, he allowed his weight to crush her against the door. "I don't give a shit what people say."

Sure he didn't. He was Cooper Bale—star quarterback, honor student, an all-American hometown favorite. He wasn't the orphaned teenager who killed her best friend on graduation night, then disappeared after her funeral. Small towns never forgot the bad.

"I just can't…" She heard the words leave her mouth, then felt him exhale against her neck. And for a moment, his body seemed to sag into her.

This wasn't fair. For the last decade, he'd been her "reason." The reason she'd moved away, the reason she'd never come back, and the reason she'd never fallen in love again.

But just the feel of his weight slumped against her while he buried his face in the curve of her neck had her caving to his request. She didn't want to—staying in this town would only drag up more memories. And she didn't know if she could endure Cooper's anger much longer.

But right now, she couldn't endure his heartache.

"Dammit, Halle." He sighed and pushed off the door, defeat momentarily cloaking his hatred—and she saw him. The old Cooper. The Cooper who loved his family, fighting for the Cooper who was undeniably broken.

But he was wrong. She didn't just owe it to Kathryn. She owed it to him, too.

As he started to walk away, she lunged forward and grabbed his forearm before he had a chance to descend the steps. "Wait!"

He hesitated, but he didn't turn around.

"I'll do it. I'll spend time with Kathryn."

For you. I'll do it for you.

She felt Cooper relax beneath her fingertips as his shoulders slumped forward. "Thank you," he whispered.

She tugged on his hand, needing to look at him—to make sure he was okay. He was so good at walking away from her. She wouldn't put it past him to continue down the steps without saying another word. It shouldn't have mattered either way, but it did.

"Cooper…"

When he huffed a sigh at the sound of her voice, she felt the color drain from her face, and she dropped his hand, her arm falling limply to her side.

God, she was such a fool to keep torturing herself like this, and now she'd just committed to staying in town to help the very man who couldn't even stand to be near her.

Instinct told her to go inside, but apparently, her better judgment was impaired when it came to this man, and she just stood there. She wasn't sure how long she remained like that before he turned around, or how long she stared at him once he finally looked at her.

Relief flooded his face, and she swore his eyes softened. She stepped into him, and when her breasts grazed his chest, his lips parted, and for a moment, she thought he was going to kiss her. And God, she wanted it—needed it even.

But instead, he pressed against her, the solid weight of his body forcing her feet to back step until she was once again strained against the front door.

"What are you doing, Halle?"

She knew his words were meant to intimidate her, but instead, they warmed flutters in her stomach as the gravelly intonation smoothed across her skin.

Holding her own, she leveled her eyes on his. "I should ask you the same thing."

His palm connected with the door, and the steel in his eyes returned. "Are you trying to test my temper? Weaken my control?"

Exasperated, she sighed. Flattening her hands on his chest, she shoved at him, except he didn't budge, not even a little. "It's obvious I don't need to test your temper when it comes to me. You've got that pretty much perfected. And if anyone's control is weakening, it's mine," she said, making sure to keep her eyes focused on his.

"You think *your* control is weakening?"

"Yes." She knew it was.

A groan tore from his throat. "You have no idea." Then his mouth slammed onto hers, devouring her as he cupped the sides of her face.

He delved past her lips and invaded her mouth, sweeping his tongue over hers. Her legs went weak beneath her as he deepened their kiss, sinking his teeth into her bottom lip while his fingertips slipped into her hair. Desperation swirled through her, and she crawled up his body, trying to get closer, yearning for even a sample of the alleviation she knew he could provide her.

Somewhere in the recesses of her mind, a warning tugged,

foretelling the injuries her reckless body would inflict on her heart. But she couldn't find it in her to stop. *This*—his arms holding her, his mouth consuming her, his body crushing her—she needed this. She *missed* this.

Grappling at her shirt, their lips disconnected, and he yanked it over her head. "I need to know why." His voice was deep, his eyes hooded as he absorbed the sight of her breasts before curving his neck down to lick the swell above her bra.

Her head thudded against the door as pleasure ripped through her.

"Why do you do this to me?" Ripples of delicious aches reverberated between her thighs as he placed an open-mouthed kiss to her breast, then slowly lifted his gaze to hers. "You're tearing me up inside."

His admission pierced her aroused stupor, and she stiffened. "I'm not doing anything to you. I—"

"Don't lie to me, Halle," he whispered, undoing the button on her jeans while his lips toured the curve of her neck.

She stifled a cry when he dipped his hips and nestled his hard length against the apex of her thighs. A slow burn fanned inside her. Her chest expanded, yet she couldn't catch her breath. The feel of his body's reaction to hers was so good. Too good.

"You know exactly what you're doing to me."

Her lids fluttered shut, her mouth went slack, and goose bumps prickled her skin as he dragged his bottom lip up to her ear and nipped it gently.

"It hurts so goddamn much to look at you, to hear your voice. And when I taste your lips," he said, peppering feather-light kisses along her jaw, "that hurt shreds me open and fucking ruins me. Over and over again."

She wanted to jolt from his arms, feeling the need to protect herself from his words. But instead, the girl inside her, who'd loved the boy he used to be, wrapped her arms around him and held on even tighter.

A lewd growl shook his chest as he took her mouth with a carnal intensity that nearly terrified her—but she didn't want him any other way. She craved his desperation. Because it mirrored her own.

Shudders cascaded though her body as he rocked into her, his cock pressing through the barriers between them.

Oh god.

She was sensitive and aching, and she wanted more.

At some point during their kiss, his hat had fallen off, allowing her to run her fingers through his disheveled hair. He'd always kept it short, but she was beginning to think she preferred it longer.

The next several seconds blurred together. He palmed her breasts, she tugged his hair, he sucked her lip into his mouth, she latched onto his shoulders and grinded against him...

Their mouths never broke contact as he pulled her zipper down, tickling her flesh as he settled his hand on her sex, his deft finger stroking her up and down in measured sweeps over her panties.

But as good as it felt to have his hands on her body like this again, she wanted to feel *more*.

And whether she could admit it or not, her body wanted his touch because some part of her still wanted *him*. Some part of her still cared for him.

A low groan resounded from deep in Cooper's throat when he slipped his fingers beneath her panties.

"Uhn," she cried, knowing exactly what his body was

going through. Just the feel of his skin on hers had her muscles relaxing and tightening all at the same time. And when he glided his fingers between her folds and sank them inside her, she went boneless.

The desire she felt from his touch as he continued to work her over with his fingers, the heel of his palm aiding with a delicious friction, was ripening, evolving, and she began to tremble.

"So tell me why I can't stop?" He crooked his fingers, finding her soft spot and caressing it with the attentiveness of a seasoned lover and the savagery of a starved man.

A moan danced over her lips, blending harmoniously with her breaths that had become pants. His voice, his touch, both soothed and provoked a trembling low in her belly, and she could feel her release blooming like a kaleidoscope of pleasure.

God, she didn't want him to stop. There was no denying his body's need. He wanted her. But his mind—his heart— felt differently. She knew this.

"Tell me why I want to pull these damned jeans from your legs and sink my face between your thighs until your taste is the only thing I can remember?"

Clenching around him, she whimpered. She wanted it. Everything his touch promised. But who was she kidding? They had too much history to be able to enjoy each other's body like this with no consequence. Their emotions were already in, and if they continued this, it would be impossible to get them out.

But she was too late. She dropped her head to his chest as ripple after ripple of bliss tore through her. She vaguely heard Cooper's appreciative groan as he kissed the side of her neck, his fingers dragging the last of her orgasm from her trembling body.

She rested her palms on his chest, pressed her thighs together, and tried to find the strength to speak. "All I can tell you is that it won't change anything. It'll still hurt when you look at me"—reaching back, she twisted the door knob—"and you'll still hate me."

"Hate you? Jesus, Halle."

As she looked up at him—all aroused and disheveled, those familiar blue eyes—she thought of the boy she fell in love with.

It was one of those walks down memory lane that made her trip and fall. Her teeth bit into her lip until she could no longer take it. She would carry the weight of Peyton's death for as long as she lived, and she'd come to terms with that years ago. But now she harbored the blame of killing the boy inside Cooper. And coming to terms with that was unbearable.

"I don't hate you," he said.

No? He just hated the way she reminded him of everything that went wrong in his past. They were hurting each other all over again. Her being here was destroying him. And she didn't know what she could do to stop it. Say goodbye to him? Pretend everything that had come back between them didn't exist? She wasn't even sure she could do either anymore.

"So where does that leave us then, Coop?"

He shrugged, then pinched the bridge of his nose before rubbing his face. He looked exhausted.

"I don't know." He paused as if he was thinking it over. "Stay. At least for a little while. Go see my mom. She needs you."

Chapter Seven

"Heads up, Miller," Cooper warned as he tossed a plastic container to Abel.

"Let me guess, Rilynn?" Abel asked, turning the container over in his hands, examining the concoction of food.

"Yeah, she brought it to the garage today. I told her I'd bring you some."

Abe nodded his head toward the construction site, indicating for Cooper to follow him. "You mean you wanted to get it out of your shop so you and the rest of the guys weren't pressured into eating anymore of it?" he asked, popping open the corner of the lid and taking a whiff. Without a second thought, he tossed it into the trash bin.

"You're damn right."

Rilynn Price worked for him at the garage. That woman could rock a pair of oil covered jeans and fix any problem under the hood of a car, but she couldn't cook to save her life. Not a chance in hell would he tell her that, though. He and the guys would swallow down whatever she brought in, and they'd do it with smiles on their faces—taking one for the team. Or quite possibly for preservation. He wouldn't put it past Rilynn to kick any of their asses.

"Well, you're not sporting a scowl today. I'm assuming things went well with Halle the other night?"

Copper just huffed and followed Abe inside the expansive frame of what was soon to be Abel's home.

He didn't feel much like delving into that topic of conversation today. Yeah, he knew Abel was curious as shit, but he didn't want to go there.

He'd spent the morning yesterday grocery shopping for his mom in the attempt that she'd find more inspiration to get back to cooking and baking like she'd always loved. When he'd delivered them to her house, he'd been surprised when she helped him put them away. Her smile was fainter than it'd been the day Halle visited her, but it'd been there. And that gave him hope.

"I told you, man. She's going to start spending time with Mom, hopefully pull her out of the fucking hole she's in."

"And you really think that'll work?"

"You saw her Saturday night, you tell me? How many times has my mom held a conversation with us in the last ten years that consisted of more than single word answers? Let alone cook a meal? Never."

"I know, you're right." Abe blew out a heavy breath and turned around to face him. "Look. You know I'm behind you. Anything to help your mom. But you weren't the only one who cared about Halle. She and Peyton were a package deal when it came to being your friend, and they were like little sisters to me, too, man. I get that you and Halle have some demons between you, but I'm telling you right now, don't hurt her. She's gone through enough."

Cooper felt the muscles in his body tighten in a domino effect throughout his back. He pursed his lips together to keep from telling Abel to shove his concern up his ass.

Who the hell did Abel think he was to claim responsibility for her?

Possessive flames licked across his flesh. "You think I don't know that?"

Abel sat down on a rectangular cooler in the middle of the concrete floor. "Chill out. That's not what I was implying."

"Think you ought to clarify then?" Cooper spat.

"We both know that woman got under your skin. She was there ten years ago, and she's still there now. The difference is, ten years ago you loved her, and now—"

"And now what? I hate her? I can't stand being close to her because I can't look at her without remembering that night. You're right, I loved her. And now…"

Now he didn't know which way was left or right, up or down.

"…I don't know whether to toss her in my bed or out of my life. Tell me, because I'm losing my shit here." He dragged his hand through his hair, his feet adopting the task of wearing down the slab of pavement along the back side of the room.

"Keep your distance. This is probably just as hard on her as it is on you. So do you both a favor and just steer clear from her."

Yeah, that was easier said than done. It'd only been two days, and his skin already itched with the need to see her again.

He'd worked so hard to get ahead of his past. It wasn't easy when all it took was one look at his mom to be reminded of how he'd fucked up. But he'd come out on the other side somehow. Sure, his life wasn't exactly what he'd thought it'd be, but he was making do.

Until Halle had shown up. Within days, she'd managed to pull him back to the past, and he feared if he went any deeper, he'd never find his way out again.

Is that a risk I'm willing to take?

He froze and fought back the urge to barrel his fist through the drywall. Because with her, he was afraid he wouldn't have a choice. She'd always been his weakness, and now was no different.

He balled his hands into fists at his sides. "I don't want to think about her right now. Show me the house."

"Well, we're behind schedule because of all the rain, so I don't have a whole hell of a lot to show you right now," Abel said, pushing up off the cooler.

That didn't matter. Cooper needed a topic change—and a distraction. No need to do any remodeling with his knuckles.

He glanced around. "This is a pretty big house, bro. This just the living room?" he asked. The frame of the house was up, the bare bones the only visual he had to go off of.

"Yeah, this is the living room, and there"—Abel motioned with his hand to the back side of the house—"will be the kitchen."

Cooper nodded in approval. "All right, show me the cave, the shitter, and where I'll be crashing when football season starts."

Abel laughed. "That would be in the basement," he said,

starting toward the front of the house where a wide staircase jutted down into a cement enclosure caged off by multiple framed rooms.

"There will be a full guest bathroom, two spare rooms for when your and Joe's drunk asses need to stay, a built-in bar, and a media room."

"Damn." He was impressed. It didn't surprise him in the least that Abel would go all out. The guy hadn't had shit for a house growing up—always said he'd build his own place one day. Cooper just didn't imagine he'd be kick-starting his own construction company, building his fucking dream house, and hiring a crew for the custom jobs he'd already started bringing in. Abel was a perfectionist, and Cooper knew that if he could, he'd build this house by himself, just to ensure it got done his way and the right way.

"Speaking of Joe, how's your brother?" Cooper asked, climbing the stairs back up to the main level.

"He comes home from Afghanistan next month. I actually hired him out to help me finish this place so he'll be moving down here for a while."

"I didn't know Joe did construction, too."

Abel laughed. "That fucker can do anything."

He watched as Abel took off his baseball hat and squeezed the bill. Something was bothering him. Growing up, Abel used to wear the shit out of his hats. It was a habit of his, and Cooper had seen it enough times over the years to know when something was wrong.

He leaned back against the doorframe of one of the rooms and looked at Abel, his brows rising while he waited for him to explain.

"I talked to him a few weeks ago, and shit, Coop, things

got bad."

Cooper didn't know Joe all that well. He and Abel shared the same piece-of-shit father, but Joe'd lucked out and had a mom who actually gave a damn. While Abel had been stuck in a cesspool trailer with his drunk father, Joe had grown up with his mom in Kentucky. Joe hadn't visited much until he was old enough to drive here himself, but even then, he and Abel had been close. Real close.

"Bad how?"

"He didn't get into much over the phone. But I figured he could use a change while he figured it out."

Cooper nodded. It didn't surprise him that Abel was trying to be the problem solver, that guy put the weight of everyone on his fucking shoulders.

"What about you?" Abel asked when they got back outside. "You gonna figure your shit out?"

Copper threw his leg over his bike and started the engine. "I'm gonna try."

Cooper's motorcycle purred to silence as he cut the engine in front of his mom's house. After leaving Abel's, he'd gone back to the garage for a few hours to clear his head, to bury his lewd thoughts beneath the hood of his old Ford for a little while. Pathetic thing was, the routine motions of tightening bolts and changing plugs only relaxed his mind and allowed him to dwell on the very woman he was trying to escape.

And Abel was sure as shit right. The only solution to whatever this thing was with Halle would be to keep his distance from her. He didn't need to pop the hood of his truck to come to that understanding.

There wasn't much in the way of restraint where she was concerned. If the way she'd felt the other night, trembling against him as he slid his fingers inside her, was a testament of his control, it was apparent his was waning.

It was easy to imagine her supple body pinned beneath him, her nails sinking into his scalp, and her long, creamy legs clenching his waist. He'd graced the depths of her tight pussy only once, but he could still recall the feel of her pleasure contracting around his cock—his sweet, untouched Halle, trembling as if she had been designed for his body alone.

Had she been with anyone else since him?

The muscles in his jaw ticked, his teeth clamping down tight. He wasn't an idiot. It'd been ten goddamn years. But the very thought that another man had been inside what he'd claimed first sent savage waves of jealousy through his veins.

I was her first, and I'll be dammed if I'm not her last.

The thought tumbled from his mouth in an audible growl that hammered the breath from his lungs.

Where in the *hell* had that come from?

His thoughts were all over the place—had been for days—and he suspected that wasn't going to change so long as Halle was the center of them. Every time he tried to come to some kind of conclusion on what to do about her, he'd remember the way it felt to have her against him—how he wanted it just as much as he didn't.

It was like trying to put together a puzzle with a missing piece. But even if he found it, the edges would be warped. It would never fit. Not with Halle. Not anymore. He was no better than his piece-of-shit father. He'd already left her once; he couldn't trust himself not to do it again. Failing her wasn't an option. Which was why he had to keep his distance.

A faint burst of laughter trickled through the crack in the front window of the house, the sound instantly drawing his attention. He held his breath, waiting for the unfamiliar noise to return, and when it did, the blood rushed from his face.

The driveway was empty aside from his bike. Glancing back to the street, he searched for Halle's car and found it parked across from the house, tucked beneath a Willow whose branches extended over the side of the road.

She was here.

The impulse to charge the front door and witness the foreign joy coming from his mother's mouth overcame his sheer fear of seeing Halle standing in his childhood home again. His strides were long as he hurried to the front door and swung it open. Then his mother's weak chortle came again, only this time it was blended with Halle's sweet sound. And his stomach dropped.

He crept down the hall, keeping clear of all the spots on the old hardwood floor that always creaked beneath his weight.

Once he reached the end of the hallway, he paused, resting his shoulder against the wall as he watched them. Halle was leaning against the counter, her back to him, humming as she chopped vegetables. Her hair was tied up on top of her head, silken tendrils whispering over her nape. Her curves clung to the thin baby pink T-shirt that draped her body while her ass filled out the jeans fastened to her hips like a second skin.

So much had changed since he'd last seen her in this

house. Hell, his whole goddamn world had tipped. But he still couldn't take his eyes off her…

"Hi, sweetheart."

He blinked and cleared his throat, the sound of his mother's voice yanking him from his momentary reprieve.

Halle's body stiffened before she whipped around, her eyes going wide at the sight of him.

"Hey, Mom." He nodded. "Halle."

"Hi, Cooper," she replied dryly before turning back to her chopping board.

His mom looked from him to Halle. He could see her concern in the frown that had begun to form across her sunken cheeks, and he quickly intervened. Not a chance in hell was he going to allow the tension between him and Halle to send his mother's smile back to where she'd stored it all these years. Not. A. Chance. In. Hell.

"So, what're you ladies fixin'?" he asked, making sure to add a little extra enthusiasm in his tone.

Instantly, his mom's worried expression relaxed a bit. "Halle is showing me a new recipe. Did you know she has her own catering company?"

No, but it didn't surprise him. He smiled to himself. Cooking was one of the things his mom had always shared with Halle. Since Peyton had hated to cook, and was horrible at it, his mom had loved having someone to teach all her family secrets and recipes to.

"Can you believe she's home?"

Home? The word grated the back of his throat like sandpaper. He supposed this was as much her home as it was his. Funny thing was, it hadn't felt like a home in years. Not until he saw Halle standing in it again.

He cleared his throat, responding with an indifferent nod, and stepped in front of his mom. "Smells fantastic, Mom," he murmured, wrapping her in a hug and kissing the top of her head.

Pull your shit together.

He crossed the kitchen and grabbed a beer from the fridge, when instead, all he wanted to do was walk up behind Halle, bury his face in her neck, and make her knees quiver beneath her.

"I'm gonna go clean up." He needed a shower and a few more long-necks. Then maybe, just maybe, he could find a way to keep his distance.

Chapter Eight

Trying to remind herself that visiting Kathryn was the right thing to do, Halle took a deep breath and forced herself to remain calm as she watched Cooper tramp down the back hallway.

It was already hard enough to be in this house, in this kitchen, going about the mundane routine of cooking dinner with the woman who'd taught her everything she knew about cooking and baking. Especially since that woman was no longer the woman she'd been before.

But to be here with Cooper in the next room was the cruelest case of déjà vu.

"Halle, honey, did you hear me?"

Blinking, she tore her gaze from the now empty hallway. "I'm sorry. What did you say?"

She nodded to the stove. "I think your onions are done caramelizing."

Reels of smoke stemmed from the simmering pan. *Shit!*

Lowering the flame beneath the burner, she stirred the onions and garlic, peeling a few unfortunate layers from the bottom of the pan.

"They're a little over-brown, but they'll be fine," she muttered aloud, more to reassure herself than Kathryn. She couldn't remember the last time she'd screwed up in the kitchen.

Then again, she never got distracted in the kitchen. Cooking was her yoga. Which made Cooper her ice cream...

Her ears pricked at the sound of pelting water streaming from down the hall.

Distracted. Yes, she was thoroughly distracted. And now she was compelled to suffer through the sound of water sluicing over a now naked Cooper.

"Do you want to help me make the sauce?" she asked Kathryn, looking for anything to revert her attention back to the task at hand.

"Sure."

"Great. Can you grab the cream and the sun-dried tomatoes?"

As Kathryn retrieved the items, Halle couldn't help but stare at the evidence of her frailty. Her body drooped as she walked, her blond hair dull and lifeless around her face, her eyes flat and hollow.

"Thank you." She feigned a smile. "If you want to go ahead and stir that in with the onions, I'll finish preparing the salad."

With a simple nod and a labored grin, Kathryn started emptying the remaining ingredients into the pan.

Although their day had been peppered with a few comforting laughs and fond memories, the majority of their conversation had been sparse. She knew the moment she saw

Kathryn the other day that loneliness had stolen her soul—and it crushed her. But witnessing her fatigue, her invariable responses, proved that the depth of Kathryn's depression was far more severe than she'd realized.

It wasn't surprising to learn that Cooper had stepped in to take care of Kathryn after Mr. Bale left. God, she still couldn't imagine that man turning his back on his wife, on his son. Growing up, she'd always pictured him as a superhero. Everyone mourned in their own way—even superheroes. But abandoning his family?

She supposed it didn't matter anymore. Cooper held the superhero title now. He was the indestructible force keeping his mother safe. He was the one she depended on. And that was the Cooper she remembered. His grief and anger had changed him, too, but he still harbored those same qualities somewhere deep inside. She had to believe that.

Tremors of guilt licked up her spine. It wasn't supposed to be like this. Cooper was supposed to be a doctor, living his life somewhere exciting. But instead, he'd given everything up to move back to this small town. He'd deserted his dream of med school so he could take care of his family that was in shambles because of *her* stupid mistake.

She didn't blame him for hating her. She hated herself.

"I think we're about done," she announced as she set the salad bowl on the kitchen table. "I just need to toss the pasta in the sauce."

"I'll do that. You go on and tell Copper dinner's ready," Kathryn replied, glancing over her shoulder.

Nodding, she wiped her hands on the dishtowel before crossing the kitchen to the back hall that led to the bedrooms. Warm steam blanketed her as she passed the bathroom. The door was still shut, but she could smell the heavenly scent of Cooper wafting through the crack beneath the door. The fragrant condensation caressed her skin, and she inhaled.

She wasn't naive enough to believe things could ever be the way they used to be with him. But there was something about being in this house and walking down this hall that resurrected the eighteen-year-old girl who was in love with her best friend's older brother.

Halle sighed inwardly, cradling her arms to her chest as she paused in the doorway of Cooper's old room. She kind of missed that girl. That girl had been full of nerves and inelegant in her own body when she'd snuck into this very room. Yet, at the same time, she'd been brave.

She wished she was brave now.

The room was empty save for his old full size bed and dresser. The bean bag chair was gone where she and Peyton used to sit while they'd watched and waited for Cooper and Abel to let them have a turn on the Nintendo. The basketball hoop on the back of his closet door was missing, and the Baywatch poster next to where his signed Colts jersey had been proudly displayed were both removed, leaving the walls naked. It was so different than she remembered.

Heat soaked into her skin, and her breath faltered. Her shirt absorbed droplets of water as the weight of a muscled chest slowly pressed against the curve of her back.

She didn't startle at the contact. Almost as if her body was prepared for him, except her heart hadn't received the memo. Her pulse hastened, syncing with the breath bathing her nape.

Cooper's lips trailed from the back of her neck to the curve of her shoulder and her body stilled. Was she wrong for wanting to savor this?

"You need something?" he murmured, the throaty gruff of his voice tickling her flesh.

She bit her lip to keep from shouting, *You, I need you*, and instead allowed herself to take pleasure in the feeling of his abs against her back, while the sharp cut of his hips pressed against her bottom.

She'd grown to appreciate her long legs over the years, but there was something to be said about the way Cooper's massive body made her feel. She became dainty and small, her curves turning supple. She hadn't even realized her lids had drifted shut until she felt his fingertips rasp up the center of her throat and her eyes fluttered open.

"What do you need?"

She had to swallow a moan. Where did she even start? "Dinner's ready," she said, her voice incapable of more than a muted whisper.

"Nah, I don't think that's what you needed, Hal."

Hal...

The way he said her name made her whimper with a longing to hear it again. No one had called her that since she'd left Glenley.

She felt her inhibitions launch into an unrelenting spiral, and she couldn't help the words that tumbled from her mouth. "And what is it you think I need?" Her shoulders bowed back, and her ass nestled tightly to him. A beaten groan clambered from his throat at the same time his thick length hardened.

"What are we doing here, Hal?" There it was again. A glimpse of the tenderness he'd always given her.

What are we doing?

She spun in his arms and gasped when she saw his eyes, like midnight navy circling crisp artic waters. "I don't know," she admitted. Though, if he kept looking at her like that, she was certain they would find out.

His large hands floated down her stomach, wavering at the flare of her hips before they dropped back to his sides. Her pulse stuttered from the loss of his touch. It was as if her hormones and her heart plummeted to the floor.

"Hal—"

She shook her head and stepped away from him. "Please don't," she whispered, raising her palms to him as he advanced into the room and shut the door behind him. "We can't keep doing this, not if it never goes anywhere." But she could hear the lack of resolve in her voice.

"I agree," he said, and the innuendo laced in his tone splintered her flesh with an intangible heat, prickling desire at her core. With each step, his chest inflated with heavy breaths, and eyes smoldered with unrestrained lust.

She watched his body transform in to a sexual temple, his leisurely steps stirring her nerves in time with her thudding heart. If he kept coming toward her, she wouldn't be able to say no.

· · ·

Cooper knew the risk, but he couldn't stop himself. Halle was here, trembling an arms-length away from him, and it set off every goddamn urge to tuck her against his body and turn her trembles into mind-blowing convulsions.

If his reaction when he'd come out of the bathroom and saw her leaning against his old bedroom door had been some sort of test, he'd fucking failed. Bad.

Her guard had been down, her vulnerability acting as a siren call to his vice. Thinking became unnecessary—*impossible*—when all he wanted to do was touch her again.

Faint lines formed at the corners of her eyes as she watched him approach her. He wished they were alone, sealed away in his house a few miles down the road. Then perhaps he could rid his body of the memory of her sheathing his cock, her slick arousal coating him as he brought her to orgasm. Maybe this was what they needed. Maybe if they could have each other's body, their hearts would let go.

Bullshit.

He was an asshole to even allow that thought to enter his mind. This was Halle for crying out loud, *his* Halle. One taste of those red lips would be all it'd take to lose himself in her again.

He stopped a single step away from her and ran his fingers though his wet hair, mussing the excess water out. Anything to distract himself from reaching out and grabbing her. "I realize we—"

"You know what, Cooper, just stop."

Pinching his brows, he tilted his head to the side. "Stop what exactly?"

A small, biting laugh escaped her. "Everything." Her hands flapped down to her sides. "Veiling all the screwed up damage between us with your wet, naked chest and come-hither eyes doesn't change the fact it's still there. Deep and ugly."

Fuck him, he wished he *could* stop. The muscles at the corner of his lips began to tighten. She was pouting—and son-of-a-bitch it was hot. His stomach burned from the laughter he was holding in as he examined the purse of her lips and the bunch between her eyes that made her look a little less angry and a lot more sexy. It felt good, almost good enough to loosen the reins and let a good chuckle slip through.

"You shouldn't look at me like that," she whispered.

"Maybe not," he said, widening his stance as he folded his arms across his chest. "But going off the way your nipples are tightening beneath your shirt right now, I'd bet it's safe to say you don't mind it."

She sighed. "Oh, fantastic, I can add mockery to the list of faults you've seemed to obtain over the years." She bit her lip. "Matter of fact, we should add the way you're looking at me to the list, too." Heat flushed her ivory cheeks, blossoming soft peach freckles into sexy little rosettes that dotted her cheekbones and spattered the creamy hollow at the base of her throat.

He had to touch her. He could list about a dozen reasons why he shouldn't, except he wasn't ready to talk himself out of it. Not that he imagined it would be an easy feat at this point.

He took the final step that separated them and lifted his thumb to the cluster of beauty marks on her collarbone. Her breath caught, and her teeth pulled on the corner of her bottom lip.

"I've got my fair share of faults." His fingers splayed across her milky skin as his thumb traced the path her freckles made down the valley between her breasts. "But I assure you, looking at you isn't one of them."

She closed her eyes, sighing sweetly as his thumb traveled back up to the side of her neck. "I want to strip you bare and look at every inch of you. Taste all of you." He leaned forward, lowered his mouth down to the dip in her throat, and then smoothed the tip of his tongue over each freckle, absorbing the way her pulse felt as it increased beneath his mouth. When he lifted his head, he had to swallow back the urgency that overcame him to slam his lips to hers. "Tell me what you want."

Hal's lids darted open, those damn vivid green eyes, fastened on his so desperately that he felt the pull all the way in his groin.

She placed her hand on his chest and whimpered, her tongue wetting her lips, mindlessly drawing his attention to where she needed it most.

But then her eyes flashed to the door, and he saw the decision turning over in her mind. She wanted to leave…

"Don't," he warned, and her gaze snapped back to his.

"Don't what?"

"Don't let me be the reason you leave again. She needs you."

Shock foisted in the widening of her eyes, in her subtle, barely audible intake of breath. This woman had burrowed a spot so fucking deep in his chest that when she'd left, it never healed. He felt her slip back in, though. Filling the space she'd once inhabited. "I'm not leaving."

"Good." He drew her even closer, her scent seeping into his pores as the fabric of her shirt abraded his chest. A growl ripped from his throat when he felt her nipples pebble.

"I'm trying," he muttered, repeating the mantra he'd found himself saying in his head a thousand times since she'd returned. But try as he might, he was a goner when her body responded to him like this.

"Trying what?"

"To keep my distance from you." He swept a wayward hair from her face. "It's a lot harder than I'd hoped."

Her eyes flashed, and he saw a woman who needed more than he had to give.

"Well, for both of our sakes," she said, pushing on his shoulders until he released her from his hold, "you need to try harder."

She crossed the room, then stopped at the door and glanced back at him.

She wanted him to try harder. He just didn't know how possible that would be anymore.

Chapter Nine

The conversation at dinner had been sparse, but his mom was finally eating something. So if it meant Cooper had to suffer through dinner with a pit in his stomach and an epic case of blue balls just so his mom would get some real food in her body, he'd do it every damn night.

"I've got this, go sit down with your mom," Halle said as she stacked the dinner plates from the table and carried them to the sink.

"No, you cooked, least I can do is help with dishes."

"Really, Cooper. I've got it."

He grabbed the empty glasses. "And I said I'm helping."

She cut her eyes to him before pulling a wine glass from the cabinet and pouring herself a glass of the red wine his mother had left out. "Okay, fine. Thank you."

The glasses clanked together as he placed them in the sink. "So, you own your own catering business, huh?"

When she turned around, she smiled, and he realized

that was the first time he'd created that reaction from her since she'd been home. She was so damn beautiful when she smiled. And he was determined to make her do it again before the night was through.

"What happened to you couldn't do small talk?" she teased, throwing his words from the other night back at him.

He flinched. "I'm sorry. Having you back here hasn't been easy on me, but I'm making an effort here."

"And you think it's been easy on me?"

"Let's not do this here." *Christ*. If this was his way of getting her to smile again, he was doing a bang up job.

Her lips pressed to the glass, and she tipped her head back, downing the wine in a few deep pulls. She rested the small of her back against the counter and licked the remaining wine from her lips. "I don't want to fight with you." She sighed. "I never wanted to fight with you."

Nodding, he dumped the leftover pasta into a container. "I hear a 'but' coming." He studied her, watching as she weighed her words in her mind before returning his gaze.

"But nothing. Peyton's dead, and I'm alive. And your mother—" She glanced to the living room where his mom was drinking her nightly glass of wine, staring mindlessly at the TV. "God, Cooper. Your poor mom. I never wanted to fight with you, but I can't blame you for hating me. Not anymore."

His stomach bottomed out, and in two quick strides he was in front of her, his hands locked on either side of her face. "My mom is my responsibility, you got me? Mine." He probed his index finger to his chest. "*I'm* to blame for her. She doesn't have anything to do with what's between us."

"Doesn't she? Isn't that why I'm standing here right now? You said yourself that I owe her."

"I say a lot of things I don't mean when I'm pissed." He brushed his thumb from her temple to her jaw. It was never his intention to make her believe his mom's illness was her doing. Never. "And I shouldn't have said that. I'm sorry. You're the one fixing her. And that's a hell of a lot more than I've been able to do."

He turned away from her. Blood swam though his veins, oxygen fled his lungs, and all he wanted to do was yank Halle to him and crush her mouth to his until the only thing he was capable of comprehending was the sound of her moaning against his lips.

He jerked when the lightest of touches circled his arm and drew him back around.

"You aren't to blame for your mother's depression, Cooper. I saw the way her eyes brightened when you walked in the room today. You're her hero."

He'd been accused of being a lot of things, and most of the time, they were true. But not this time. "I'm no hero, Hal."

She lifted her fingers to his clenched jaw and ran them across the stubble he'd developed since that morning, the velvet touch compelling his eyes to shut.

"Look at me," she demanded, and even if he wanted to, he couldn't deny her that one simple request. "Peyton's death changed us, maybe even you most of all. You might not be the boy I grew up with anymore, but you're still the hero, Coop. I promise." She cupped his cheek and dusted his lips with her thumb. "You're still the hero."

If she even knew how wrong she was…

He didn't deserve her compassion, and he sure as hell hadn't done anything to deserve her comfort. But there was no mistaking the way it soothed him.

• • •

Halle watched from the kitchen as Cooper carried his sleeping mom to bed as if she were a toddler. She wished things were different for him and Kathryn, but she couldn't help but feel a warmth cocoon her at the sight of him taking care of his mom. He was so careful with her.

With the house so quiet, she felt like an intruder. And that just reaffirmed how different things were now. Not that she'd forgotten, or that she ever could, which only made it feel that much worse.

Thankfully, the weight of the evening seemed to lift a little when she walked into the backyard. The fresh air whipped around her and she inhaled, grateful for the sound of the breeze as it swished through the trees.

Her laugh flooded the night as she looked up and saw the old tree house, if it could even be classified as one. It rested maybe five feet from the ground and was supported by two by fours as opposed to the tree's branches. Peyton had wanted a tree house so badly, and she would've loved nothing more than to have it at the very top of the tree if it were possible. But when her dad finally agreed to build it for her, she insisted it be low to the ground. Because Halle was afraid of heights.

After testing the ladder's hopeful strength, she climbed up and sat down, her feet dangling over the edge. The night was calm, though a bit chilly, and it didn't take her long to get lost in the stars like she had so many times before. It wasn't until she'd heard Cooper's voice that she noticed him standing in front of her.

"I thought you'd left for a minute there."

"Nope, still here." She peered at him and tried to get a read on him. "Unless you want me to leave?"

Without acknowledging her question, he stepped up the ladder, then sat down on the platform next to her. His thigh pressed along hers and the contact, though nothing more than a casual brush, had tingles erupting on her scalp. She'd been reduced to a hormonal teenager. Wonderful.

Several minutes passed as they sat there, silently, just staring out into the darkened yard. Awkward came with the territory. Years of pent up guilt and anger combined with the craving she was feeling at that very moment was the exact recipe for awkward. Surprisingly, though, it didn't last long, and she found herself relaxing next to him.

"Thanks for tonight," he said, his voice whipping through the quiet.

She turned to look at him, but his eyes were unfocused as he glanced ahead. "You're welcome."

"I'm not just talking about my mom, Hal."

Then what exactly *was* he talking about? When his eyes found hers, she held her breath and waited for him to explain. Instead, a slight smile turned up one corner of his mouth. She should've known an explanation would've been too much to hope for, but his lopsided smirk was almost better, and she couldn't help but return one of her own.

"I thought I was going to have to work for that."

Eyes creasing, she asked, "For what?"

"Your smile. It's been a long time since I've made you smile."

God, how was she supposed to resist this man? She

swallowed down the sentiment of his words and shook her head, playfully rocking her shoulder into his. "If I remember correctly, you were always pretty good at it."

"That was a long time ago." His body stilled next to her. "A lot has changed."

She didn't want to push him, but considering the tension visible in his body, she feared she already had. Biting her lip, she offered him a nod, then smiled again. "You're right," she said. "But not *everything* has changed."

Like the way her stomach somersaulted when he was close to her, or how when he looked at her like the way he was at that very moment, her heart picked up a beat or two.

When he finally broke eye contact, he stood and sighed. "I haven't been up here in years," he said, ducking his head as he peeked inside.

A board creaked beneath his feet and sent Halle scrambling away from the ledge. Had she not been terrified, she would have reveled in the way his deep chuckle bathed the air around them and prickled goose bumps on her skin.

"I see your fear of heights hasn't changed."

He belted out another laugh when she narrowed her eyes. "Unfortunately, not," she said, taking his offered hand.

In the second it took for him to pull her up and place her between him and the tree house, safely away from falling to her untimely death, she was already nestling her body to his. How could she not when he cracked that grin and pressed her against him as though he couldn't get her close enough?

He tucked a strand of hair behind her ear, his thumb lingering on her cheek. "Halle Morgan," he said as if he was just now seeing her for the first time. "Ten goddamn years." He shook his head. "I'm not sure how in the hell I've made it that long without you."

She sucked in a shallow breath, her heart stalling as if she was afraid to feel the full force of his words. And she was. But they were damn good words.

He licked his lips as he studied her, his hips nestling against her, his arms enveloping her. She resisted the unrelenting urge to pull his mouth down to hers, and instead allowed him this moment. Whatever this moment may be.

"God, I've missed you. I just didn't realize how fucking much until now."

She couldn't breathe. His words had always been her undoing. And right now, it was in the best possible way. What was she supposed to say? It would be impossible to count how many nights she'd wondered the very thing he'd just confessed. She didn't think there was a word created that described just how terribly she'd missed him.

He missed me.

Then all too soon, he stroked her bottom lip with his thumb, then stepped back. "Come on," he said, before climbing the few steps down to the grass below. He quickly and easily grabbed her by the waist and lifted her from the platform. Instinctively, a soft squeal trickled from her mouth as her feet left solid ground. With a shake of his head and a chuckle that made her insides thaw, he set her down.

"So much fucking harder than I'd hoped," he muttered to himself, placing a hand on her lower back as he guided her toward the front yard.

When they rounded the corner of the house and stepped on to the driveway, she had to force her feet to move one in front of the other. Given what he'd just said to her, the last thing she possibly wanted right now was to leave. But maybe this was for the best. She'd allowed herself to get wrapped up in the familiarity of the night, hell, of the whole damn day—in his words. If there was one thing she'd learned about this new Cooper these last few days, it was that he had a short fuse. She didn't want to push him.

Cooper helped her into her car then with his arms propped up on the door, he leaned down, that half-smile, half-smirk making its appearance. And she found herself wishing he'd change his mind and ask her to stay with him.

But instead, he thumped his hand on top of the car. "Be careful driving home."

Chapter Ten

"I'm sure, Courtney. I have to do this," Halle said into the phone, tucking her legs up beneath her on the couch and popping the cork on the cheap bottle of wine she'd picked up on her way home from Kathryn's.

"All right, if you say so. I'll take care of things here. Don't worry."

After spending the day with Kathryn, she knew she needed to stay. Kathryn wasn't well, not by a long shot. But Halle couldn't deny that their time together was doing Kathryn good. All the more reason to stick around a little longer.

"Mmph," she moaned as she gulped down some wine. "Thank you. Seriously, I owe you one."

"Nah, it's no big deal. We've got that big wedding next Saturday at the Ivory Gardens, but I'll recruit a few extra hands to help me prepare, and we'll be fine."

Shit. She'd forgotten all about the Jameson wedding. Hors d'oeuvres and a full course dinner for over four hundred guests. There was no way she could miss that event. "With everything going on, I completely forgot."

"Look, honey. I don't know what all you've got goin' on right now in that town of yours, but I know that if you don't stay and try to figure it out, you'll be kickin' yourself in the ass about it later."

"I know, but—"

"Maybe you forgot this little detail, but I own half of the business, too. I think I can handle a large event on my own."

Courtney was right. She was completely capable, and their staff was excellent. Halle had nothing to worry about. "I know, I know."

"Good, then it's settled."

"Just don't forget about the—"

"Gluten free menu, yes, I know."

She laughed. "Okay."

"So you want to tell me the real reason you're staying?" Courtney asked.

Halle choked on the sip of wine she'd just taken. Clearing her throat she asked, "What?"

"Oh, come on, Halle. You've been hiding from that Podunk town for as long as I've known you. Be honest. How much does this stay have to do with Cooper's mom, and how much does it have to do with Cooper?"

Be honest? That was a tall order…

"I'm staying for Kathryn. If it wasn't for her, I would have already been home by now."

"But…"

Halle sighed, not sure if she was grateful for Courtney's canny way of reading between the lines, or annoyed. "I don't know. It's just…maybe if I…God, Courtney…"

"Maybe if you help his mom move on, Cooper will forgive you?"

A relieved breath heaved from her chest as Courtney revealed the words she was too afraid to say herself. "Yeah."

"You can't put that pressure on yourself."

"You don't understand. He's broken… And it's because of me."

"I'm going to stop you right there," Courtney said, her voice piercingly sharp. "None of this is your fault. You were a kid who made a stupid decision, a decision that your friend made as well. You might've left town, but he was the one who left you. You can't—"

"You should see the way he looks at me, Court," she interrupted, refilling her wine glass to the brim. "I knew he would be angry. But there's something else. I can't help but wonder what if…" She heard Courtney sigh, and Halle took a long sip of her wine while she waited for the lecture to start in.

"Do me a favor," Courtney said. "Please don't let this man break your heart all over again."

That was it? No pep talk about her worth or what she did or didn't need from a man? No rambling list of Halle's finer attributes? She was a bit disappointed.

She set her glass down on the coffee table, her elbow clumsily hitting the tin box that was still sitting there, and it toppled to the floor. *Dammit.*

"Halle? I'm not kidding."

"I won't," she promised, glad to know Court hadn't wimped out on her best friend chats.

"That didn't sound too convincing."

Sighing, she leaned down and started gathering the dis-arrayed items on the floor. "Sorry, I just dropped…"

Her brows pinched together as she picked up a large zip-lock baggie. "Hey, I'll call and check in a few days, okay?" she muttered as she opened the bag and pulled out an old Notre Dame football T-shirt—Cooper's T-shirt.

"Is everything all right?

"Yeah, fine,"

After saying a reassuring good-bye, Halle dropped the phone to the couch. She'd forgotten all about this T-shirt. Peyton had taken it from Cooper the morning they'd buried the box. She'd wanted to put his dream in their box, too.

Bunching the shirt to her nose, she inhaled, searching for a small trace of him. It was odorless, nothing but the scent of plastic and cotton filling her nose. She draped it over the coffee table, then returned to her glass of wine, draining its contents while she stared at the shirt.

The alcohol was failing miserably in its effort to occupy her mind with thoughts other than Cooper. Instead, she was consumed with them. His mouth on her neck, his hands digging into her hips, his erection nestled against her ass. She crossed her arms and narrowed her eyes at the shirt. It was silly, really. To want to cover her body in an old, worn-in T-shirt just because it had once covered the very body she was struggling to remove from her imagination. But her intoxicated conscience didn't give a damn about frivolousness.

She staggered to her feet and stripped down to her panties, stumbling around as she kicked her discarded clothes to the side of the couch before sliding the shirt over her head.

The fabric glided across her naked body and hung off her shoulders like a cape, the sleeves covering her elbows, and the hem falling mid-thigh.

She brought the collar to her nose. God, she wished it

smelled like him…

The roar of an engine reverberated through the walls of the house, and she stared in the direction of the front door as if she could see through layers of drywall and brick. The rumbling purred for a few more seconds before the noise cut off. Her breath froze in her lungs as she waited for the inevitable knock on the door.

Cooper was here.

• • •

Cooper didn't know what made him turn his bike down Halle's road and pull onto her driveway. But here he was.

He'd been on his way home, attempting and failing to use the ride to cool his body and clear his head. The next thing he knew, he was cutting the engine in front of her house.

A dim florescent glow illuminated the house through the shaded windows. If he knew what was good for him, he would start up his bike and drive the hell away from there that very second. But that was the problem, he couldn't.

He pulled off his helmet and shook his hair out of his eyes. He'd let her leave to keep from taking her home with him, to keep some fucking distance, and now he was here, back in the line of fire.

His fingers dug into his pocket and pulled out his phone. It was almost ten. Surely, she wasn't asleep yet.

The image of her tucked on her side, tangled in the sheets as her hair spilled out around her pillow saturated his mind's eye. Raw, primitive urges plummeted though him, and he climbed off his bike and jogged up the porch steps before he even realized he'd moved.

But just as he lifted his hand to knock, the door swung wide open. Halle stood before him, her hip propped against the door, her thighs pressed together, and her body covered in nothing but his old Notre Dame T-shirt.

Fuck.

His deprived gaze gripped her the way his hands suddenly itched to. God, he loved the way she looked in his shirt. Molten need ripped him apart as he took in every graceful inch of her thighs. Some greater power had a hand in his self-control, because if it was up to him, he'd have already yanked it from her body so he could see what lay beneath.

His scrutiny finally fell to her face, and he watched as she swallowed, her cheeks flushed with arousal and nerves. He didn't just see the lust in her expression, he *felt* it. Like it was tethered to his own, rooting her longing in his damn soul.

Her tongue moistened her parted lips, drawing his attention to her Cupid's bow. His restraint was already paper-thin, if she kept that up, he'd lose it completely.

"Hey."

Her eyes remained guarded, but he saw the quickening of her breaths. "Hi."

"Can I come in?"

"I don't think that's a good idea. Besides, I'm getting ready to go to bed."

A tortured groan silently shook his chest, and he closed his eyes. "Fuck. I'm not sure telling me you're getting ready to crawl in bed is the best argument if you don't want me to come inside."

"Cooper..."

He opened his eyes and stepped into her, his chest maneuvering her out of the way as he crossed through the doorway.

She stepped aside, but her hand was still on the door as if she wasn't exactly sure what else to do. "What are you doing here?"

He laughed. "I'm not real sure."

Timid eyes blinked at him, and her teeth grazed the corner of her bottom lip, sketching blueprints in his mind of things he'd do to those lips given the chance again.

Slowly, he blew out a heavy breath and scrubbed his hand down his face. "I'm tryin', Hal."

"Okay." She nodded. "Good."

Good? He didn't suspect anything was *good* at the moment, and the way her voice rattled when she spoke made him believe good was far from what she was feeling. He wouldn't blame her if she told him to take a hike. But he wasn't ready to leave, not yet.

"What's wrong?"

She began shutting the door. "Nothing."

He frowned and tipped his head to look at her. It might've been ten years, but that didn't mean he didn't recognize her ticks when she was uneasy. Her lips pressed together, and she gathered her hair to the side, mindlessly twisting it like she always used to do.

"Bullshit, babe."

Her eyes widened at the endearment the same moment his balls tightened. The word caressed his tongue and rolled off his lips so effortlessly; it felt fuckin' right.

"Start talking," he demanded.

She lowered her gaze and tugged on the hem of his T-shirt in a futile attempt to cover her exposed thighs.

He arched his brows. "It's nothing I haven't seen before."

And it wasn't anything he wouldn't mind seeing more of.

"No kidding," she quipped, rolling her eyes. "It's just—"

"My old shirt?"

She nodded and her face blazed crimson. She'd been caught red-handed, voluntarily wearing his shirt.

He trailed his gaze painstakingly slowly down her body again. She squirmed, and he watched as her thighs brushed together, her nipples hardening beneath the thin cotton. When their gazes locked once again, he whispered, "Looks good on you."

Wetting her lips, she looked away and put her hands on her hips, nodding down the hall. "Um, come on in. I'm going to go change, then we can talk?"

"I don't know if I'm ready to talk," he said, following her down the hall. She looked back at him and frowned, probably because he couldn't take his eyes off her ass. "And I'd really rather you not change."

"Coop," she chided.

With a sigh, he smirked and shook his head. "Jesus, Hal. You've got my head so fucked up I…"

She wrapped her arms around her middle and waited patiently for a few heartbeats while he tried to sort the shit in his head. But it was a lost cause.

"Say something," she whispered.

He squared his shoulders. "I'm not sure you want to know what I've got to say."

"Try me," she said, but he didn't miss the nerves quaking her voice.

One deliberate step was all it took for him to rid the space between their bodies. Before she could change her mind, he slipped his fingers into the tangles of her hair and tugged her closer. "It was one thing when you were off living your life away from this town, away from me. I could keep my distance. But now, dammit Hal, I can't. Not when you're right fucking here."

The corner of her mouth lifted in a smile she couldn't hide. "Okay. Well," she said, looking down at their bodies pressed tightly together. And when she met his gaze again, her smile reached her eyes. "I think you've covered the distance thing."

Giving her a crooked grin, he said, "No, babe. I haven't."

Her little intake of breath unraveled his control, and he took her hand and kissed the inside of her wrist. His whole body throbbed with the need to touch and explore her.

A breath grazed past her lips as her body sank against him. After everything, she still trusted him. She'd surrendered herself to the hell between them and trusted him to pull her from its depths when this was over.

The pang in his chest reminded him that he might not be able to. But then the fire in her eyes burned away all of his hesitation.

Screw the consequences. He'd deal with the fallout tomorrow.

Chapter Eleven

"You need to tell me right now if you still want me to try harder to stay away," he murmured, his lips brushing hers.

Halle sucked in a quiet breath, hoping her heart would find its way back to her chest. He was giving her an out, an opportunity to close the door on whatever was about to transpire between them.

"And if I tell you I don't want you to try at all?"

Panic thudded in her chest when a groan vibrated in Cooper's throat. It was a primitive sound, one that resonated in her core and promised so much more than she thought she was ready for.

Cooper pushed her hair behind her shoulders and licked his lips. Yes, god yes, she was ready for this—she needed it.

Seconds passed, and she didn't know if he was giving her a chance to change her mind, or if he'd already changed his. Then his knuckles fluttered down her sides and explored the skin below her belly button.

"Then I'll lay you in bed, strip you bare, and relive the memory of the first time I had you. The memory that branded us both." Leaning down, he nipped her ear, kissed it soothingly, then whispered, "I'll make you come hard, and I'll make you scream loud. I'll bury myself deep inside you, and I won't stop until we've created a new memory."

She closed her eyes at the heavy promise in his words. Cooper's body bowed over hers, the muscles of his lower back tightening and dancing beneath her splayed hands. "Will we survive it?" she breathed as his lips brushed the side of her neck, his nose nuzzling the curve until he found just the right spot to press his lips.

A somber whisper hesitated on his tongue. "I don't think so, Hal." The warmth of his breath bathed her with the truth. This would hurt, and there would be no coming back from it. She knew without a doubt that regret would follow, and that it would forever taint her memory of Cooper.

Her bravery had been flawed for so long, but not anymore. She knew the repercussions of his touch, and she understood the risk.

"Then I don't want to survive anymore."

His head snapped up. "Babe…"

As she raised up on her toes, she pressed her mouth to his. He didn't move as she tended to his bottom lip, then his top, licking, and sucking, and nibbling.

It was as if a switch had been flipped inside him, and everything happened at once, leaving her mind trying to play catch up with her body. Cooper groaned, his mouth parted, his tongue claimed hers, and the next thing she knew, she was in his arms, being lowered onto her bed.

He tugged her T-shirt up with his teeth. "I think about

it, you know."

Her breathing halted when he stopped to nip at her belly button, dipping the tip of his tongue inside. "About what?" she asked, not sure if she cared for the answer or not. She just didn't want him to stop the blissful torture his mouth was putting her through.

"Your body beneath mine. The way you felt when I pressed into you, that sweet, innocent barrier that gave just for me. And those goddamn lips that ruined me."

"Ohh," she breathed as the flat of his tongue followed the path his fingertips made to her breasts, and then he wrenched her shirt over her head.

Vivid images of a smooth faced Cooper attentively loving her for the first time played out on a video reel in her mind. She hadn't had a clue as to what she was doing, but with Cooper, it had felt easy...perfect.

He was right about one thing, though. He wasn't the same guy who'd tenderly taken her virginity. The man above her now had aged with strength, marred roughly by the hand he'd been dealt, yet still as callously beautiful as he was ten years ago. His tenderness was replaced with desperation, but it was a feeling she feverishly welcomed.

His body was harder, and it contoured to her curves like a custom mold created just for her. The scruff on his jaw tickled her skin as his mouth continued to dance along every square inch of her stomach, the plane between her breasts, and the peaks of her nipples.

An urgency that had been festering since he had her pressed against the building of the bar ripped through her. "Clothes. Off. Please," she managed to say in between arching her back and rotating her hips, hungrily seeking out some sort of relief.

His fingers slid beneath the thin strap of her panties, and without lifting his lips from her skin, he ripped them off in one swift tug. The heady groan that left his lips fanned tiny flames of pleasure between her thighs.

He leaned back and pressed his palms to the inside of her knees, parting her legs until they dropped to the sides. He appraised her, his eyes worshiping her with a calculated hunger, as though he was savoring the very sight of her.

Helplessly exposed to him, she began to squirm beneath his gaze. "Cooper," she urged.

He wet his lips. "Hold on tight, babe."

Before she had the chance to process his words, his mouth descended, and his tongue greedily ravaged her sex with swift, long strokes.

"Ohh." Her fingernails clawed at the sheets, twisting the cotton in her hands while Cooper devoured her, sending her hurtling toward her climax. A finger swirled at her opening and she pinned her hips to the bed. "Please don't tease me."

"Oh baby. That's exactly what I plan to do." His pace slowed, and his lips hovered over her clit as his hooded eyes flitted to hers. "It's been ten years since I've tasted you. Ten years since I've been inside you, and I'll be damned if I'm not going to draw this out and make it last as long as I can. And I plan to drive you insane while doing it."

Oh God.

The threat sent delicious, painful vibrations straight to her core. "Please, Cooper. I can't stand it."

"No." He pushed the tip of his finger into her, and her walls clenched down on him, trying to pull him in deep. She felt him smile against the inside of her thigh. "If I only get this one last time, I'm going to make it count."

Oh, hell.

As if he heard her rampant thoughts, he lifted his head and delved his fingers into her slick sex. "I claimed this, baby. You gave me this beautiful, untouched body a long time ago, and I'm going to make sure you remember long after tonight just how good I can make it feel."

It was certain. After tonight, she would never be the same.

Only right now, she didn't care. One more night with him would be worth it.

• • •

Halle's honeyed arousal bristled Cooper's senses. Her lush, feminine musk combined with her taste sent all the blood in his body straight to his cock. All he wanted was to sink balls deep inside her pussy and destroy her thoughts with the friction of his thrusts until she couldn't remember her own name.

But he didn't.

Not yet at least.

Right now he was going to bring her to orgasm by his mouth alone, and he wasn't going to make it easy on her.

Sucking her clit between his lips, he waited until he drew a delirious whimper from her mouth before he let go. She writhed and bucked and tore her hands through his hair—but she didn't come.

He grinned.

"God, Cooper. I can't... Please... Uhnnn... Don't stop." Her airy cry was a second away from daggering his resolve.

He loved the sound of his name pleading from her lips.

"Just let me have my fill of you first, and I promise, when I let you come on my tongue, it'll be more than worth the wait."

Throwing her head back onto the pillows, she balled the sheet in her fists, locked her knees behind his neck, and whined. And it was the most tempting sound he'd ever heard.

His little game of pleasured torment continued a few more rounds as he brought her to the brink of orgasm, then let her fall slowly back down, only to repeat it over, and over, and over...

When a sheen of sweat glistened over her body, and when her legs began to quiver uncontrollably, he thrust his fingers deep inside her, curving them just...where...she... needed...

"Cooper!" she screamed.

"That's it, baby." He watched her features morph with pleasure. Her hips rocked, grinding herself against his face as she dropped her head back between her shoulders. "Uh-uh. Eyes on me."

Lazily, she raised her head and lifted her lids, pure ecstasy ripping through her. "I'm so close," she panted.

"I know, baby. I know."

Keeping his eyes locked on hers, he swirled the tip of his tongue over her clit while stroking her with the pads of his fingers. Her mouth rounded, her eyes fought to stay open, and then her body convulsed. And it was fucking beautiful.

As he slowed his fingers to a leisure caress, she fell back onto the bed. "That was... Oh my god... You're... That was..."

Withdrawing from her, he smirked. "Well worth the wait?"

Her eyes glassed over and she sank her teeth into her

bottom lip. "God, yes."

Laughing, he stood up from the bed and peeled out of his clothes, knowing damn good and well he would have her saying that again before the night was through.

Halle elongated across the mattress—legs stretching, toes pointing, and lips purring a soft moan.

"Even more beautiful than in my memory."

Her eyes blinked open and she gasped, the appreciative little noise reaching down and grabbing him by the balls. Hearing her breathy desperation awakened the longing he was trying so damn hard to ignore. The one reminding him that this woman had taken ownership of his heart ten years ago and had never given it back.

Licking her lips, she scanned his body, her eyes falling over his erection before meeting his gaze, then she rose to her hands and knees and crawled across the mattress to him.

His cock swelled even more at the sight of her. Moonlight poured in through the slants in the blinds, illuminating her skin with an angelic glow, reflecting the golden strands in her hair like a halo.

"So damn beautiful," he breathed.

She stopped in front of him, leaned back on her heels, and peered up at him from beneath her lashes. He kissed her—hard. He couldn't help himself. Their moans blended, tongues swirled, and lips bruised while he gripped her hips, pulling her flush against him. He was desperate for her— every inch of her.

Ten years.

There was little he could do about the thought once it entered his mind. Of course he was desperate for her, it'd been so long since he'd had the privilege of seeing and feeling her naked against him. And honestly, he couldn't remember a day that had gone by that he hadn't felt her absence.

Now she was here, tucked against him, and there was no fucking way he could ever get enough of her.

Shards of ice formed in his chest. He knew first hand there was no known way to rid the need for this woman from his body. If he knew how, he would have done so years ago to save himself from the torment of missing her. But letting her go was the real issue, and he didn't know how it was going to be possible after tonight.

It took every morsel of strength in his bones to remove his mouth from hers, and when he did, she whimpered in protest.

"Lie down."

Pressing her lips together, she shook her head. "Not yet."

"Now, Halle." He coasted his knuckles across her stomach and tried to savor the way she shivered. "I don't just *want* inside you. I *need* inside you. Now." He breathed.

"Not yet," she whispered across his jaw, reaching between their bodies and wrapping her hand around his cock. "I want to make it count, too."

Her fingers tightened, and his head dropped back on a groan. Then he felt those goddamn perfect lips wrap around his sensitive head, her warm tongue blazing across the flare of his cock with measured flicks, and he lost all semblance of being. He only existed on the realm of pleasure her mouth encased him in.

Thrusting his hands into her hair, his hips jerked, and his jaw clenched as he hit the back of her throat. Holy hell, what was she doing to him? He began to pull back, but her hands reached around and latched onto his ass, holding him in place as she sucked him deep.

Tingles erupted at the base of his spine, pressure built, and his body tensed. She was going to kill him.

"Babe," he implored, pulling her hands from his body.

She hummed her disapproval, her lips tightening around him as she slid back down to the hilt.

"Fuuck," he hissed. "As much as I want to come in that hot mouth of yours, that would put a flaw in my plan to draw this out. And I'm nowhere near done with you."

The little vibrations her mouth made as she moaned were testing his restraint...and his stamina. She slid her mouth up his cock and swirled her tongue one last time before removing her lips.

In an instant, he was on top of her, securing her body to the mattress. His lips on her shoulder, he lapped at her skin, indulging in the way her taste settled on his tongue as he held himself over her.

Her tight entrance cradled the head of his cock, and anticipation flared inside him when she pressed her thighs against his hips. He lifted his head and held her gaze. "I don't want anything between us while I'm inside you. I want to feel you, warm and wet and bare—clinging to me. Nothing but you, babe."

He'd never made love raw before, never spilled himself inside a woman. But with Halle, he *needed* it. Needed to claim her in this one small way—to make her his, to feel her completely.

Her eyes went hazy with lust, her teeth pulling on her lip as she gazed up at him. "Yes. I'm protected," she assured, answering his unspoken question. Rocking her hips, she nodded. "Plea—"

The word didn't finish sliding off her tongue before his hips rolled forward and he pushed inside her.

Blissful warmth sheathed him, her pussy tightening around his cock as she slowly stretched, welcoming him completely.

With her hands clinging to his back, and her fingernails digging into his flesh, she lifted her head from the pillow and crushed her mouth to his. Jesus, he'd been deprived of this—of her—and now that he had her, was inside her, he felt their past tear through him, reminding him just how right and perfect and…Christ…it reminded him of what it felt like to feel something other than the constant anger and pain and guilt.

If heaven was tangible, this was it: right here, right now, wrapped inside the only woman who had ever consumed him.

"If kissing you ruined me, then being inside you is bound to fucking kill me," he breathed across her lips. He wanted to make this last until their bodies were spent and depleted. Then make love to her again. He pulled his hips back, and with every slow inch he dragged his cock from her body, she clung on that much tighter.

"Tonight," she whispered, her thumbs stroking his cheeks as she stared into his eyes, "how about I soothe you instead?"

Fucking hell.

He wrapped his arms beneath her knees and thrust hard inside her. She gasped, pulling in a sharp breath as the tip of his cock stroked her G-spot. "That's my job," he said, lifting his hips, then plunging back inside her. "Let me take care of you."

Then he kissed her, and all the tenderness he'd wanted to

give her fled from his body when she closed her lips around his tongue and sucked it into her mouth. The starved man inside him groaned in approval, and his hand moved to grip the nape of her neck.

Their mouths set the pace, his hips rocking into her with the same impetuous greed. He laced his fingers through hers and slid her arms above her head. And when she squeezed his hand, it was as if she'd reached inside his chest and squeezed his heart.

"Cooper," she murmured. She licked the seam of his lips, then slowly traced the perimeter of his mouth. "Take me. Don't hold back." She opened her eyes and held his gaze. "Please."

Lust swirled in her eyes, desperation softening her muscles in a silent offering. She was giving herself to him—again. He sure as fuck didn't deserve her—not her body, not her mouth, and no way in hell did he deserve this power. But he was selfish, and he was going to take what she was offering him.

"Sit up," he coaxed, pulling her toward him. His cock throbbed as it slid from her hot channel. "Now, turn around."

Without hesitation, she rose to her knees and turned her back to him. His fingers tweaked her nipple as he palmed the swell of her breast, reveling in the way goose bumps flared over her entire body as he kissed her nape and splayed his hot breath across her skin.

"You trust me?"

She nodded. "Completely."

Though he knew with every facet of his being that he didn't deserve it, he couldn't stop the satisfaction that erupted in his veins. He gathered her hands behind her back and snaked his free arm around her stomach, anchoring her hips to him, and supporting her weight.

"Lower your shoulders to the bed, baby. I've got you."

She complied, and it was so sexy. The soft nubs of her spine dotted her back as she lay with her cheek on the pillow, her ass in the air, and her hands secured in his.

• • •

With her face nestled against the down pillow and her arms pinned behind her, Halle was subject to Cooper's touch, to his scrutiny, and it darted pricks of passion straight to her core.

She felt his weight lower over her, and the tendons in her arms pulled as her shoulders bowed back against the pressure. Then she felt his mouth branding her with open-mouthed kisses, and her eyes drifted shut on a moan.

"You okay?" The vibrations of his words caressed her skin like velvet, though the sound that hummed around her was strained and rough—sexy.

"Yes," she whispered.

"Good."

The calloused pad of his finger stroked over her clit, the feather light sensation hurdling through her. "No more teasing, please," she begged.

He growled, mercilessly delving his fingers into her sex. "This isn't me teasing you, baby. This is me savoring you," he said, withdrawing from her, smearing her arousal up between her folds. "All these years I thought I'd painted you in my mind, memorized the way your naked body looked trembling from my touch, the way your pink pussy glistened with need for me. But I was wrong. There's no possible way to capture this perfection. No memory will ever do you justice."

She felt his cock nestled at the apex of her thighs as he bent over her again, and she felt like she could combust from the anticipation.

"But I promised you a new memory, didn't I?"

She gasped as he seated himself inside her in one swift thrust.

"No memory can ever come close to this, baby. But I'll try like hell to give you one."

When he pulled his cock from her sex, she shuddered, the friction drawing a long moan from her throat. Her spine arched as Cooper leaned back into his thrusts. His hips pelted her from behind, his tempo increasing with every slap of flesh. She couldn't move; she was prisoner to him as he deliciously abraded her. Heat blazed in her belly and sent flames spreading hot and fast through her core.

"Oh God. Cooper…" This was what she wanted, for him to let go, to take her—uninhibited, intense, and dirty.

A low, heady grunt was his response, followed by a hard thrust that ricocheted pleasure all the way down to her toes.

"So tight." Thrust. "So wet." Thrust. "So warm." Thrust. "So. Fucking. Perfect."

Pressure built as he continued to pound into her. Her body rocked from the impact, her face crushed against the pillow, her shoulders digging into the mattress.

"Fuuck," he groaned, reaching around, finding her sensitive bud, and massaging it with his thumb. "It's never been this good, never—only you, babe. Come with me."

She was so close, she didn't need the demand, yet the way his voice strained with his own approaching release pushed her to the brink. "Oh…"

"Louder. I want you to be loud."

His words grated her body, and she screamed, moaning and crying his name in a stream of incoherent pleads. His body jerked hard with one last, quick stroke, his cock sinking to the hilt as warmth coated her deep inside.

Once he released her hands, he collapsed onto her, his heavy pants bathing her neck. A few heartbeats passed as they collected a semblance of strength, then he pulled her up and cradled her against his chest.

Her body felt boneless, and she wasn't sure whether she'd be able to move even if she tried. So instead, she rolled her head back onto Copper's shoulder and allowed him to hold her upright.

"Mmm," he moaned, nuzzling the curve of her neck. "Come here."

As if she were weightless, he scooped her body against his and lay them down on the bed, tucking himself behind her.

Just as he had earlier, Halle tried to savor the moment, but the lingering waves of pleasure began to steal her consciousness. She was encased in comfort, in safety. And for the first time in ten years, she felt like she was home.

• • •

It took a moment for Cooper's eyes to focus in the dim morning light. Laying there with Halle tucked against him, he waited for regret to slam into his chest, but none came. All he felt was Halle's soft breath.

Careful not to wake her, he softly traced his fingers along her back and absorbed the way she curled into him. It'd been so long since he'd felt something this good. He was used to banning memoires from his thoughts, and this woman right here, she held them all. The good, the bad, and every single one in between.

Halle sighed, and the way she tangled her body around his and held on tight made him feel as if he was the very force keeping her on this earth. And all he'd offered her was one goddamn night? He knew the reason why, but he didn't want to think about that now. There were a few more hours of dawn before morning would creep in and steal the day from them.

Slowly, he unraveled her limbs from his, then pressed a light kiss to her shoulder. Her sleep induced moan as she folded into the mattress stirred his already hard cock.

He quietly slid from bed and pulled his jeans on. If he texted Rilynn now, there was a good chance she'd see it when she woke up and would know to open the shop up for him today. Because there wasn't a chance he'd be coming in on time. Not when he had more time with Halle—naked and sleepy.

Unable to help it, Cooper glanced back at Halle before he stepped out into the hall. The soft hues of blue that were caught between night and day draped her fair skin and illuminated her copper hair.

No memory even comes close.

Eager to get back in bed and cover her body with his, he walked a few paces down the hall to the living room so not to wake her. But just as he was punching in a quick text to Ry, he froze. His fingers stilled, and his feet cemented in place.

The pit in his heart felt like it was opening up and swallowing him whole.

Photos upon photos were scattered everywhere. Notes,

an old perfume bottle, and a couple CDs all laid on the floor next to Peyton's old cheerleading pompoms and a dried up corsage that had tumbled beneath the coffee table.

Thoughts whirred on a loop in his mind, thoughts marred with memories he wanted to have, but ones he wasn't ready to endure.

This…this right here was the very reason he avoided Peyton's old room. He couldn't bear seeing the life that was gone, spilled out before him—memories trapped in pointless fucking keepsakes. The familiar telltale sign of his approaching anger crept through his chest until the ache flourished and splintered into rage.

If only I'd answered my goddamn phone…

He dragged his hand over his face. Then before he even realized he'd moved, he was back in Halle's room. His eyes gaze to her as if pulled by some greater power, and he sucked in a heavy breath. There was never any good without the goddamn bad.

His hands balled at his sides. Why had he even left her bed? If he hadn't, she'd still be tucked against him.

God, he wanted her. Wanted to stay here and hold her until their pasts were no longer visible. Except that wasn't reality. And the reality was, if he stayed, he would hurt her. Look at what his dad had done to his mom, what *he* had *already* done to Halle once before. It was inevitable.

With his jaw clenched, he pressed a light kiss to the top of her head, careful not to wake her, then slowly slid from the room.

"I'm sorry," he whispered.

Quickly and quietly, he got dressed and left, telling himself that this time, for both their sakes, he would keep his distance.

Chapter Twelve

Fifty hours at the garage this week, another eight messing around on the old Ford, and two grueling hours every night spent beating his body to hell at the gym—and Cooper was still wrung tight.

Turning his headlights off, he rolled his truck to a stop in front of Halle's house, the same as he'd done every single night since he'd walked out her door a few days ago.

He couldn't see her again, it wasn't an option. He knew that. Not that she would even want to see him after the way he'd left her after she'd fallen asleep in his arms. But here he was, on the opposite side of the street in front of her house.

He rolled down the window and took a deep breath. It eased him some, but not enough. The urge to tear out of the truck and barrel though her front door was still there.

The light in the front office window flicked off, and he glanced at the clock on his dash. Just after eleven, right on time. Seemed to be her preferred bedtime, and he'd gotten so used to seeing that little assurance that she was home and safe that it only added to his deranged need to sit outside her house every night like some fucking stalker. But just as sure as seeing her wasn't an option, neither was staying away.

With more force than necessary, he shifted the truck into drive, but just as he was lifting his foot from the brake, a dull glimmer of light flashed in the corner of his eye.

It was Halle, silhouetted by the sheer curtains draped over her bedroom window. She was merely a shadow against the florescent glow, but that didn't stop him from soaking up the sight of her.

He wasn't an idiot. He knew after feeling her body naked and needy come undone around his cock that he'd never be able to watch her move again, or look at the way she twirled her hair, or see her part her sweet cherry lips into a smile…

Not without guilt shredding him open from the inside out, and not without hurting her.

So instead, he was going to take this opportunity to sample this small bit of her from a distance.

As he watched her begin to dance in front of the window, a sharp pang squeezed his chest. Dammit, it was so familiar. He couldn't possibly count the number of times he'd watched her awkward, long legs stumble around a room to annoying-ass music as they were growing up. And though she'd grown out of her clumsiness, she was still as horrible of a dancer as when she was a scrawny thirteen-year-old.

Seconds passed and turned into minutes before her light flicked off and he was left staring into the dark. Seeing her carefree and happy, even for just that brief amount of time, rocked him to his core. She deserved to be happy, deserved a man who could undoubtedly give that to her. And that man wasn't him. Not anymore.

Because you fucking walked away.

He slammed his knuckles into the dashboard. He was a coward, just like his old man, unable to protect the women he loved….hurting the woman he'd been in love with since she crawled in his bed all those years ago. Fuck, he'd loved her long before then.

His tires kicked up dust as he peeled away. Yeah, he was an epic asshole, for hating that she blew back into this town, shifting the debris from his past into his path. And for wanting her.

• • •

She'd survived. Only slightly unscathed, her heart taking the brunt of the damage, Halle had withstood two full weeks back in Glenley.

Looking over at Kathryn, she smiled. The amount of improvement she'd shown in just the last week was unbelievable. She'd gained some weight, and some of the old brightness was beginning to return in her eyes. She just couldn't help but fear that her presence, replacing Cooper's absence, wasn't going unnoticed.

She knew he was only trying to keep his distance. Still, her heart sank a little. He'd left her—again. Even though he'd warned her, it didn't prevent her from feeling like the air was knocked out of her lungs when she'd woken up alone.

And the shitty part of it all? She missed him like crazy.

She shook her head and cursed her heart. Missing him hadn't done her any good the last ten years, and it was safe to assume it wouldn't now, either.

"I think that's good for today," she said, taking off her gardening gloves. "We better get this mess picked up before the rain comes."

Halle had picked up some perennials and a couple of hanging baskets at the farmers' market that morning, and she and Kathryn had spent the last few hours transforming her barren landscaping into a lush flower garden. It was beautiful, and though it didn't quite look the same as she remembered, it was beginning to feel more like home.

"Do you remember that time you girls snuck out of Peyton's window?" Kathryn asked as she closed the bag of potting soil next to her.

Their conversations were still mostly one sided, so Halle was surprised by Kathryn's question. "Um." She laughed. "Which time?"

A smile tugged on Kathryn's mouth. "I think you girls were maybe fifteen."

Ah, fifteen. The summer she and Peyton had fallen hopelessly in love with the Folten twins.

"Yeah, I remember," she said, smiling as she thought of them jumping out of the window to go play flashlight tag. Although everyone knew playing tag was code for holding hands and stealing innocent kisses with boys between houses.

"I probably think about that moment the most," Kathryn said.

When Halle heard the crack in Kathryn's voice, she stopped stacking the empty pots and looked at her. "You do? I didn't even realize you knew about that night. How come you never told us?"

"Oh, I'd planned to scold you girls when you got back, but when I heard you both talking, I couldn't bring myself to do it."

Peyton had tasted her first real kiss that night, and Halle had felt the excitement flutter in her own chest as Peyton revealed every sweet moment of it.

"I stayed up for hours that night, listening to you girls giggle and cherish the memory of Pey's first kiss. I couldn't take that away from you—or me."

Halle turned her head and wiped a tear from her cheek she hadn't even known was there. She hadn't thought about that night in years. They'd stayed up for hours, eating popcorn and doodling Peyton Claire Folten and Halle Jo Folten on nearly every page of her English notebook. Dreaming of one day being sisters-in-law, living next door to each other, and watching their kids become best friends, just as they were.

Without hesitation, she wrapped her arms around Kathryn and squeezed. It was so nice to remember the good for a change. And although Halle and Peyton hadn't realized it, Kathryn had been a part of that special moment. "You sneaky woman. Thank you for giving us that night, and for reminding me how good it was."

Blinking rapidly, she shelved the memory. Regardless of Cooper, she owed it to Peyton. If spending every evening with Kathryn, cooking and cleaning and baking ungodly amounts of sweets would help pull her back to the person she once was, then it was worth anything and everything she had.

"Are you sure you don't want to stay for dinner tonight, Halle?" Kathryn asked as they carried the potting soil and gardening tools to the shed.

"Oh, no thank you. Not tonight. I have a couple of things I need to take care of for an event I have coming up," she lied. Courtney was seamlessly and singlehandedly running the business without needing any help from her. Truth of the matter was, if she was here, then Cooper wasn't. Halle could see Kathryn needed him to be here, too. He might not believe it, but he was helping her just as much as Halle was. How could he not see that?

It wasn't quite noon yet, and fortunately, the heavy clouds that threatened rain had stayed away while they'd planted, but as she put the last of the supplies in the shed, a drop landed on her shoulder, then her cheek. Saying a quick goodbye with a promise to see Kathryn tomorrow, she jogged to her car and reversed out of the driveway, just as the clouds opened up.

It wasn't unusual weather for the end of May in Indiana. She was used to it. Besides, there was always something about the rain that felt cathartic. Storms could be unpredictable and terrifying and complex. But with the rain, no matter its intention, she could count on the sound to lull her mind into submission and cradle whatever emotions were stumbling around.

Except the rain was failing her now. No serenity came with the patter of drops. Nope, just the reminder of the way the rain had sounded as Cooper had her pinned against the brick building of the bar.

Great. Stupid rain. The last thing she needed right now was to crave his touch. But that ship had sailed. Even if she believed she could withstand another night in his arms, he'd made his intentions crystal clear.

One night.

She just wished the night had lasted a little longer.

Mindlessly, she turned onto the desolate street that led to her house, and the next thing she knew she was screaming. Her car hydroplaned a couple of feet before her front tire found refuge in the giant pothole near the shoulder. A thud, a pop, and a few panicked heart palpitations later, and she was officially stranded on the side of the road, in the rain, with a flat tire.

Fucking fantastic.

As if sitting there and staring out the rain-blurred windshield would somehow catapult her back in time to when her car still remained balanced on four wheels, she fixed her sights ahead of her and counted to ten. She'd heard that helped in scary situations, or was that when you were upset? Either way it was unsuccessful.

If she were home, she'd call Courtney or a neighbor to come rescue her. But she was on her own here. Kathryn wasn't an option, and she sure as hell wasn't calling Cooper. She supposed she could ask Abel for help if she knew how to reach him, but she didn't.

Taking a deep breath, she stepped out into the rain and inspected the damage. She wished she'd paid more attention when, shortly after Peyton had turned sixteen, Mr. Bale had taken them out to the garage and taught them how to change a tire. But that was almost twelve years ago, and when it came to automotive lessons, her memory was a little rusty.

"Stupid pothole," she muttered, kicking the deflated tire. As she popped the trunk and pulled out the spare and the jack, she prayed to God she could do this.

The tank top she had on was soaking wet and clung to her skin like a suction cup, and her coral linen shorts weren't any better, but thirty minutes and a cramped hand later, Halle had changed her flat tire. Yet, as she got back in her car and started it up, she feared that'd been the easy part.

With a quick glance over her shoulder, she turned her car around and headed toward the only auto garage in town.

Chapter Thirteen

"Hey Ry," Cooper hollered as he stepped out of his office, glancing in the waiting room before heading into the garage. He turned the music down and chuckled when he noticed it was set on the country station. With his mechanic Dilly on shift today, he expected the speakers to be vibrating with some heavy rock tunes. The shear fact that the top forty country countdown was playing told him that Rilynn had once again suckered Dilly into it.

"Did you happen to put in an order for that part we needed for the Michelson's car? His son is leaving for his senior trip next week so I want to make sure we get it in in time."

Lifting her head from beneath the hood of a Volkswagen Bug, Rilynn pushed her bangs across her forehead and narrowed her eyes. "I put it in three days ago. Why?"

"I couldn't find the inventory sheet saying it was filled. Just wanted to make sure."

"And you assumed I forgot?"

"Uh, yeah." He'd learned fairly soon after hiring Ry that if it was misplaced, or missing, she was the first person to ask.

"Gee, thanks boss."

"Sorry, sweetheart. You'd forget your ass if Dilly over there didn't remind you of it every damn day."

Dilly flipped him off.

Cooper laughed and returned the gesture. "And I'm putting Michelson down for new brakes, too, but that's on me."

Ry leaned her hip against the car. "Yeah? I didn't know he needed any."

"Eh, they're not too bad, but the way he drives, I'd rather him have new brakes before he heads to Florida." And with their oldest son leaving for college soon and a new baby on the way, he knew Michelson was pinching pennies.

"All right, got it. Unless you want to put it on a sticky note and tape it on my forehead."

"I can do that," he said. "Now get back to work." He turned the volume up on the radio before he walked back inside.

The inventory papers scattered across the desk as Cooper tossed them aside and dug his phone out of his pocket. He checked the time like he was stuck in an hourglass. Work barely kept his mind distracted from thoughts of Halle. And the only thing that made it bearable was knowing he would be able to drive past her house again tonight and wait for the assurance of a damn light flickering off to let him know she was still here.

He realized how screwed up that sounded in his mind, but at this point, he didn't give a flying fuck. She'd been here two weeks already, and his mom was showing significant improvement. He didn't know how much longer Halle would stick around before she got back to her life away from this town. Away from him. After ten years without her, he'd thought he never wanted to see her again. Now he couldn't stand the idea of her leaving.

The chime from the front door sounded, shaking him from his thoughts. "Hi, what can I do for...?" Glancing up from his phone, his mouth went dry. "Halle? What the hell happened?" he asked, rushing around the desk to where she stood by the front door, soaked from head to toe, lips chattering and skin prickled with chill bumps. "Are you okay?"

Without hesitation, he wrapped his hands around her elbows and pulled her body in close to his so he could inspect her.

She frowned, watching him as he scanned her body. "I'm fine. Just wet. My car hydroplaned, and I hit a pothole pretty hard. Blew out my tire."

She hydroplaned?

Dammit, he should have paid more attention to her car before he and Abel had dropped it off at her house the first night she was back in town. It'd been here at the garage for Christ's sake, he could have easily checked her tires and replaced them, inspected her breaks. But he hadn't. He'd been too distracted by her homecoming, too intoxicated by the smell of her lingering on his skin, and too pissed off to think straight.

"Why didn't you call me?" he asked. She had no business changing a flat in this weather. She could have lost her damn hand or gotten hit by a car.

Her expression morphed into shock. "You can't be serious."

One brow lifted as he tipped his chin down. "As a fuckin' heart attack," he growled.

"You know exactly why I didn't call you." She jerked from his hold, looked around the empty waiting room, and whispered, "Look, I knew the other night... What happened between us... I understood that was all it would be, only one night."

"That doesn't mean you couldn't have called me. Jesus, Halle. You could've gotten hurt."

She closed her eyes, and when she opened them again, it was as if she'd finally accepted that he wasn't the man he used to be. "I'm not an idiot, Coop. It's not like I expected anything to change." She sighed. "I guess I should be used to it by now."

"Used to what?"

He blanched when she just shrugged and laughed. "You. Walking away. Take your pick," she whispered, the sound so quiet he barely heard her.

Son-of-a-bitch. Walking away from her had been the last thing he'd wanted to do. And trying to keep his distance these past few days.... That'd been impossible.

Just as it was impossible to keep from reaching out and smoothing away the cluster of hair that was clinging to her neck. Her eyelids fluttered closed on a sigh as his fingers danced across her skin, her spiked lashes sending residual droplets of rain down her cheeks.

His muscles tightened. He shouldn't be doing this. But every nerve in his body ached to feel her, and he didn't care anymore.

This was *his* Halle, softening beneath his touch. Just the way he liked her.

Her eyes remained closed, and her breaths deepened as her mouth fell open, her body mindlessly leaning in to his.

His cock hardened, his heart pounded, his blood heated, and tasting her sweet breath on his tongue became a necessity.

He felt a tug, like whiplash in his chest, as his eyes drifted over her lips, and the need to kiss her — to show her just how badly he couldn't keep away — won out.

"Don't," she pleaded, the sound stopping him before he even had the chance to change her mind.

His hands dropped to his sides as if she'd electrocuted him. Shit, the single word might as well have done just that.

"Holy shit, it's pouring out there. If this rain keeps up, I'm never gonna make any headway on the house," came Abel's voice over the sound of the door chime and the beating of water on the roof.

Cursing under his breath, Cooper stepped away from Halle but never removed his gaze from hers. "Abe, think you could give us — "

"Halle, you okay?" Abel asked, once again interrupting Cooper as he stepped up beside her.

When she turned to Abel, her eyes warmed. Cooper's muscles turned rock hard and white-hot envy leaped up his spine. He couldn't win. No matter what he did, he was damned. Hating her tore him open, but loving her... Loving her had wrecked him in the best and worst possible way.

"Is someone going to tell me what happened?" Abel snapped as his eyes roamed over her, inspecting for injuries, much like he had.

Abel was as good a man as they came — he was his best friend — but that didn't prevent the tick in Cooper's jaw from tightening, or stop him from clenching his hands at his sides as the lick of possession snaked through his body. Narrowing his eyes at his friend, he stepped in front of Halle.

Able glared back as if sending him a silent "fuck off" before looking over his shoulder to Halle. "What the hell happened, Hal?"

He felt the casual shrug of her shoulders from behind him. "Nothing serious, just a flat tire."

"And you changed it by yourself?"

"Yes. Is that really so hard to believe?"

Cooper choked back his smirk as he imagined her drilling holes into Abel's head. And by the deflated expression on his buddy's face, she was pouting, too.

"Why didn't you call—?"

She sighed. "Not you, too, Abe."

Abel nodded. "I take it Coop already gave you this lecture?"

"For the most part."

"All right, fair enough." He took a step back, pulling his wet baseball hat off and tossing it onto one of the waiting chairs. "You need any help, brother?"

"Yeah, I do. Man the shop for me while I take Halle home, will ya?"

"Sure."

Halle shook her head. "I'll just wait while you replace my tire. It's no big deal."

He pinned her with a look he hoped would halt any potential pouting, regardless of how sexy she looked when she pursed her lips.

"Not happening. And don't fucking argue with me, because we both know it won't work. You're going home and getting out of those wet clothes." He wanted her warm and dry. Not to mention he couldn't stand the thought of anyone seeing the body that was on display beneath her wet shirt. He was about to gouge Abel's eyes from their sockets as it was. "I'm all out of extra T-shirts, so unless you want the one off my back—which I'll gladly give you—I'm taking you home."

Her eyes widened as they grazed the length of his torso, sweeping across his chest and shoulders. He swore he saw her tug on her bottom lip with her teeth, but as quickly as it took for her to take an affected little breath, she looked away.

Sighing, she adjusted her purse that was strapped across her shoulder and started toward the door. "Fine. Let's go then."

Walking past Abel, he nodded his thanks.

"Hal," Abel called out as Cooper was opening the door for her.

Pausing, she glanced over her shoulder. "Yeah?"

"You comin' to Beer Fest tomorrow?"

Leave it to Abel to open his damn mouth. Cooper pummeled back the urge to shed a few choice words at his friend.

She laughed. "You're kidding me. They still have that?"

"Hell yeah. You remember Dillon Thomas? Dilly? He pretty much killed the competition with his brew last year."

"Dilly makes beer?" she asked, laughing again as she looked to Cooper for confirmation. He'd witnessed about ten different emotions cross her face in the last ten minutes, and he'd have to admit, seeing humor in her smile was the sweetest one yet.

"You laugh now, but wait until you try it," Abel said.

"What time does it start?"

"It kicks off around six or so, but it goes on all night. Good food, good beer, good company. What do ya say?"

Jesus. Wasn't Abel the one rambling his bullshit about

him needing to keep his distance from Halle, and now he was inviting her to the festival? Irritation rippled through Cooper's body, and he rolled his shoulders. "I don't think it's a good idea for you to go."

Her head whipped around to him. "What? Why not?"

"Never mind, let's go."

"No. Not never mind." Her slender fingers dug into her hips. God, what he wouldn't give to replace her hands with his, and kiss the pout from her lips. "Spit it out, Coop. What's the problem?" she asked, raising her eyebrows.

What was the problem? The last thing he needed was to see Halle's ivory skin flushed from the combination of alcohol and the heat of an early summer night while drunk assholes hit on her. No way in hell did he want her there. His temper and his restraint couldn't risk it.

When he didn't answer, she shook her head and stomped past him and out the door.

"Thanks, asshole," he said to Abel before following her out in to the rain.

Chapter Fourteen

The short drive to Halle's house was borderline torture. Even then, Cooper took the long way around town and lessened his lead foot. The mixed aromas of spring rain and the scent of lavender that wafted from her body had him shifting in his seat. Damn, she smelled good.

He tried to initiate the conversation they needed to have close to twenty different times since he pulled out of the auto garage, and now that he'd turned down her driveway, time had run out.

After throwing the truck in park, he killed the engine and shifted his body to face her.

Slowly, she turned her head toward him. "Is it really that hard to be near me? Is that why you don't want me there tomorrow?" she asked, folding her arms across her chest.

"If you honestly don't know the answer to that question, then it's probably for the best."

Her exasperated sigh filled the cab of his truck. "That's a

bunch of crap. I don't know what more I can say, what more I can do." She pushed open the door and started to get out. "I should have never come back here."

He jerked forward, grabbed her hand, and pulled her back into the truck. "Stop," he ordered, his voice unwavering as he hauled her next to him. Letting her leave like that wasn't an option.

Their eyes locked, intensity scaling his body. Her chest expanded against his, and she took a haggard breath.

"It should have been me," she said. "I *wish* it was me."

He took her by the shoulders and held her far enough away that she could see his face. "What did you just say?"

"I should've died that day."

She said the words with such conviction that it made him feel sick. He looked at her, really looked at her, then reached out and grasped her chin while he enveloped her with his body. "Don't you ever say that again. Do you understand me?"

A mewled whimper escaped her, and if he hadn't already been damaged, that sound would have wounded him. "It's true. Peyton should have lived, not me."

Baring his teeth, he let the anguish that coated his very essence hum over his lips. "I told you not to say that again."

"But it's true. Look at you." She ran her hand down his cheek. "Your heart's broken," she cried. "Don't you think I would take her place if it meant saving her? Saving you?"

"And you think if you'd switched places with Peyton, if you'd died, my heart wouldn't be broken? Dammit, Halle. You're right. Seeing my sister's body on that road haunts me every day of my life. But when I got the call that you both were in an accident and the paramedics were on their way, do you know whose face flashed to my mind first? Yours. And seeing you lying broken and bruised in that hospital bed replays in my dreams every goddamn night. So don't you for one second think that if you'd died instead of her, my heart wouldn't be broken. Because it would have been shattered—irreparable."

And there it was, his deep-seeded guilt hidden in the facets of his soul, poured out to the woman who'd slayed him ten years ago.

"If I could trade my life for my sister's, I would in a heartbeat. But I would *never* trade yours." Her eyes were unwavering, holding his with an intensity that clutched his heart, and when she finally lowered them, his heart stopped.

Warmth seeped into his skin as he dropped his forehead to hers and splayed his hands on the sides of her neck. He closed his eyes. "Babe," he coaxed. "Never."

Her breath caught in her throat, and she leaned into his touch, her eyes closing on an exhale. He felt a weight lift from his chest as she relaxed against him. All he could see was *his* Halle, not the woman who'd devastated his world, but the girl who'd made it better.

Thick, heavy tension and a silent dialogue hung between them. Seconds, minutes—eternity—passed while he inhaled the breath she released. Words turned over in his mind of what he wanted to say to her, but nothing was right. He was exhausted, torn in two straight down the fucking middle.

Finally, he allowed his hand to fall to her knee, his fingers splaying on the inside of her thigh. Her eyes flashed to his hand, her breath slipping as his fingers crept up her leg and slid beneath the hem of her shorts.

"Being near you hurts so goddamn bad that I swear,

sometimes, I can't breathe when I look at you. But staying away from you has been the hardest thing I've done. You consume me. My thoughts, my body, my broken heart. You take over my dreams, and you haunt my nightmares. There's a lot of hatred inside me, baby. It lurks like a dormant beast, and being near you feeds him. But that's not why I stayed away from you."

The thin, supple skin at the hollow of her throat pattered violently with the vibrations of her pulse. Her legs swept together, confining his hand between her thighs, and he groaned when he felt the liquid heat through her dampened panties.

"Then why?"

"Because I don't want to hurt you."

• • •

Halle dropped her head back against the seat and sighed. "That's a bullshit answer, Coop."

All at once, his hands were on her waist, and he was pulling her onto his lap. "It's the truth." He settled her on top of his thighs, her center pressing against his firm cock. An ache instantly clenched inside her, and she had to rest her hands on his chest to keep still.

He reached behind her and tugged on her ponytail until she tipped her head back. "I can't be near you without wanting to touch you," he said, dragging his thumb over her lips and down the center of her throat, "and I can't touch you without wanting to kiss you." Leaning in, he peppered the side of her neck with light kisses until she trembled. "And I sure as hell can't kiss you without wanting to make love to you," he murmured as he flicked the tip of his tongue along the skin below her ear.

Gasping, she tilted her neck to the side, offering it to him. "Is that what we did, made love?"

"Babe, there's no other way to describe being inside you," he said, lifting her shirt above her head and tossing it on the seat. He skimmed his lips across her collar bone, over the swell of her breasts and said, "I could fuck you right now," — then he slowly licked her cleavage — "hard and fast. Here in my truck, in the middle of the day," — and kissed his way back up her neck — "and I'd still be making love to you."

He rocked his hips, his erection rubbing against her clit through the layers of clothing between them, and she had to bite her lip to keep from crying out. "You're my Halle," he whispered, pulling her bottom lip from her teeth. "You always have been."

The moment a moan left her throat, their mouths crashed together, teeth tugging, tongues licking, lips bruising. She arched her back and slinked her body against his chest, rolling her center over his erection again and again. At some point, her bra found its way to the floorboard along with Cooper's shirt. She felt crazed, and powerful, and so, so, good.

"Are you going to make me rip these goddamn shorts off you, or are you going to be a good girl and take them off for me?"

Keeping her lips on his, she smiled and maneuvered herself up enough to pull her linen shorts down. She'd barely slipped a leg out before her panties were shredded from her body.

She gasped. "Impatient?"

"I didn't say anything about your thong," he said, wasting no time pushing two fingers inside her. The sensation was so intense she nearly lost her balance.

With her head thrown back between her shoulders, she pressed the small of her back against the steering wheel for leverage as she moved in rhythm with his strokes.

"Oh, damn baby, you're drenched."

She moaned and bucked her hips above him.

"That's it, ride my fingers. But don't you dare come."

"What?" she breathed, rolling her head forward to look at him.

His mouth twitched with a smirk. "When you come, my cock will be buried inside you, claiming every second of your orgasm."

Peering at him beneath hooded lids, she nodded. "Now. Then do it now." She fumbled her fingers over the waist of his jeans, silently cursing the small amount of time it took her to undo the button and slide the zipper down. But the sound that tore from his chest as she wrapped his cock in her hand made it worth it.

Withdrawing from her sex, he positioned her over the head of his erection. Pleasure shot through her center as he lowered her onto him. Slowly, she took him inside her, inch by perfect inch, until she couldn't take anymore.

She didn't have much strength left in her—she was too close. With her nails digging into his biceps, she rested her forehead on his and released a low whimper.

"You need to come, baby?" he asked, his thrusts coming hard and fast.

"Yes," she cried, pushing against him, angling her body so the tip of his cock hit her G-spot. Every. Time.

"Lean back."

As soon as her back was against the steering wheel, Cooper's thumb was on her clit. Unlike his relentless thrusts, his touch was gentle, and the different stimulations tumbled her over the edge and through her orgasm.

She held onto his thighs and screamed through ripple upon ripple of flourishing aches that never lessened. Oh my God. She was going to come again.

"Cooper," she cried out, her voice quaking.

"There's my girl." His finger never let up its slow, rhythmic caress, but his hips moved harder, faster, driving his cock inside her.

This time, when her orgasm hit, she was too spent to even hum a moan. Instead, she collapsed onto him and buried her face in his neck.

Cooper's grip tightened on her waist. "Fuck," he growled, then his release spilled inside her.

When his body finally stilled, he folded his arms around her and kissed her shoulder. "See what you do to me?"

Did he not know what he did to her?

She lifted her head and smiled. "I'm pretty sure that was all your doing."

"No, babe. You do this to me. When I'm around you, I don't just feel the bad. You make me feel the good. And I don't fucking know how to feel one without the other—how to separate the memories. I can't give you more than that."

"I don't need anything more. I didn't before, and I don't now. I just need *you*."

He rubbed his hands up and down her back and shook his head. "You shouldn't."

"Why not."

"Because you're still holding on to the man I used to be, and I'm not that man anymore."

"He's in there somewhere," she said, and then she kissed him.

He squeezed his arms around her and groaned as she slipped her tongue between his lips and tangled him in their kiss until she could no longer breathe.

Gasping, she finally pulled away. "So what now?"

"Now, I go back to work," he said, shifting her to the seat next to him.

Her heart fell to her feet. Clumsily, she pulled her shorts back on and searched for her bra. She couldn't believe she'd actually thought something had changed between them just now.

Forgetting about her bra, she slipped her wet shirt over her head and opened the door, ready to bolt toward the house. But before she had the chance, Cooper grabbed her hand and kissed her.

"I'll see you tonight."

Her eyes widened. "You will?"

His lips curved up on one side of his mouth, then he started the truck back up. "I can't keep my distance from you, baby. Not anymore."

Chapter Fifteen

After spending the entire day cleaning the house and indulging in a little comfort baking, Halle had officially eaten her weight in sweets, and, if she wanted to, could've done so off the now spotless kitchen floor.

Waking up in the middle of the night to Cooper sliding in bed with her, played part in her good mood today. So did waking up this morning with him still next to her.

She'd tried to rid the thoughts running rampant in her mind, the ones that made her wonder if this was what life could've been like. But it was silly to even entertain those thoughts. She knew better than anyone that the past couldn't be changed. As much as she wanted to, she couldn't rewind time and wake up next to Cooper every day. She couldn't bring Peyton back. All she could do now was hope like hell Cooper could move past his demons—move past the mistake she'd made all those years ago—and move forward. With her.

The faint ringing of her phone sounded from down the hall, and she quickly shuffled to the kitchen. It was in here somewhere. Searching around a counter full of sweets, she finally found her phone hidden beneath a batch of cooling sugar cookies.

"Hello?" she answered without looking at the screen.

"Hey, stranger."

An instant grin formed. "Hey, Court." Halle should've known it was her. It'd been a few days since Courtney gave her one of her infamous, meddlesome chats.

Listening to Courtney's unsolicited advice was usually among her list of things to avoid, but seeing as she was in a good mood, she figured she'd indulge her.

"What're you doin'?"

Halle looked around her kitchen at all the desserts and laughed. "Just a little baking."

"How many batches?"

Brows bunching, she asked, "What?"

"How many batches of cookies did you bake?"

Silently, Halle counted the stacks of cooling trays crowding her countertops. "Six…"

A worried sigh sounded through the phone. "Any chocolate cake?" Courtney asked.

"Chocolate cake? Yes…" she trailed off.

"Spill it," Courtney snapped. "What's wrong?"

Halle leaned against the counter and folded her arm across her chest. "Nothing's wrong. Actually, I was having a pretty good day, thank you."

"You can't lie to me, Halle. Something's bothering you, whether you realize it or not. You don't marathon bake for nothing."

She shifted her focus to the ceiling for a brief moment, then said, "Really, I'm fine. Kathryn is doing better, and Cooper and I made some progress yesterday, and this morning."

She clenched her legs together as the memory of Cooper, waking her with his mouth between her thighs, rolled through her mind.

"You little minx. You seeing him again tonight?" she asked.

"There's a beer festival here in town tonight, so I'll see him there."

Nerves kicked up in her chest and her stomach rolled.

The festival. Me and Cooper. And everyone else in town.

She swallowed hard. Maybe Courtney had been on to something after all. Because the realization that the entire town would see her with Cooper suddenly made her feel sick. What would they say? What would they think?

The last time Halle had been around anyone from town was ten years ago, when they'd paid witness to her and Peyton's fight. A fight about Cooper. Or more accurately, a fight about Halle being with Cooper…

"Halle?" Courtney's voice pummeled through her thoughts. "You okay?"

"I don't know," she admitted.

"Anything I can do?"

Halle sighed. She'd been on her own for so long now that she didn't need someone to hold her hand. But if she was going to face this town again, it would've been nice to have a wingman.

"I don't think so," Halle said, mentally trying to shake her worry and ease her stomach. She changed the topic. "How's everything going? How's the team doing?"

"Nice dodge," Courtney muttered under her breath. "Everything is fine. I told you I had it all under control here. And the team is fine. It's like they don't even realize you're gone."

Halle snorted. "Gee, thanks."

"But I do." Courtney sighed. "You need to hurry up and get your butt back home. I miss you."

Home?

She wasn't quite sure where that was anymore.

After a few more minutes of catching up with Court, she was finally able to get her off the phone.

She started the shower and stood under the pelting water until it ran cold. Enjoying a night of beer and music wasn't going to kill her. It was time she faced the past, too.

Quickly, she scrunched her hair and allowed her copper curls to fall wild and wiry. Knowing Cooper would be at the festival made her want to slip into something sexy and make him ache by sight alone. Seeing as she'd only packed for a short trip, she didn't have much in the way of clothing options, so she decided on a simple, cotton maxi dress with a subtle neckline that revealed the top swells of her breasts. If she was really going to throw herself to the wolves, she might as well feel good doing it.

When she stepped outside an hour later, her nerves had calmed a bit, and she'd convinced herself that she was worried about nothing. Besides, if all else failed, there would be plenty of beer at her disposal to get her through the night.

She climbed in the car and moaned when she smelled the heady spice of sandalwood mixed with the scent of rain and sweat. Butterflies started to take flight in her stomach as the masculine aroma wrapped around her, almost as if

Cooper was touching her.

Scared as she was to be back in the public eyes of the town, she was even more excited to see Cooper again.

As she grabbed her keys from the cup holder, she noticed a folded scrap of paper at the bottom. That familiar heart pounding began thudding in her ears as she opened the note.

Hal, really? Not only were your tires bald, but your break-pads were shot and your oil was low. You're lucky you were asleep when I got here last night. I had half a mind to wake your ass up and pull you over my knee for being so damn irresponsible. Call me next time. I'm not kidding.

She could picture him as he wrote this—eyes hard and angry, jaw locked, powerful legs parted and unwavering. It was as if she could feel the ripples of muscle in his back and hear his labored breaths as he imagined doing the very thing he threatened. His seductive warning caressed her body before the other words on the paper registered with her mind.

Wait, Cooper had done all that work to her car? Yet she knew the answer before the question flitted through her thoughts. It'd been him. Of course it had. Even now, after everything, he was still looking out for her.

The realization made the lingering hurt he'd inflicted the last few weeks thrive until it cut the circulation from her heart—tiny needles numbing it with a thousand painful pricks. This new Cooper was unpredictable. Hot and cold, on and off, push and pull. It was exhausting. And she couldn't help but worry how he would react when she showed up at the festival tonight.

Inhaling a deep breath, she threw the car into reverse and backed out of the driveway. There was only one way to find out.

Glenley hadn't changed a bit. The road was crammed with car after car parked along the curb of Main Street, and the brick road surrounding the square had been blocked off for the festival.

Her sandals clicked against the bricks as she made her way through the crowd. Laughter and chatter ensued around her, and a live band was playing cover country songs on a small makeshift stage set up on the lawn area of the square.

Food tents loitered the sidewalks, permeating the air with the warm smell of brisket, barbeque, and every possible fried food imaginable. Dozens upon dozens of brewery booths were set up along the curb, each housing their exclusive beers, claiming superiority as lines piled up in front of them.

She ignored the curious heads that shifted her way as she passed. Everyone knew everyone in Glenley, but with the locals from neighboring towns here for the festival, she was confident she would pass off as just another familiar face. Or at least, she hoped.

Taking it upon herself to join in the festivities—and knowing she'd need a little liquid courage—Halle stopped at one of the shorter lines and bought a hard cider from a woman who appeared as if she'd been better suited for brewing tea instead of beer. But one sip of the apple flavored heaven and she was proven wrong.

"Halle Morgan?"

Whipping her head to the side, she snickered at the overweight teddy bear giving her his best Copenhagen smile.

"Little Halle Morgan, I don't fuckin' believe it." He laughed, slapping his thigh.

"Dillon Thomas, looking handsome as ever." She winked. So much for thinking no one would recognize her.

"Get your ass over here, girl," he said, pulling her in and enveloping her in a suffocating hug—and it was perfect. She'd forgotten how much she loved these tender-hearted guys that had always dawdled around Peyton's house at any given hour. Dilly had been there almost as much as Abel had. Everyone had always gravitated toward the Bale house. It was safe and comfortable. It was home.

Eyes crinkling, Halle smiled. Dilly probably loved Kathryn's cooking more than she had.

When he finally released her, his elbow bumped her plastic cup as she pulled her arm from his round waist, and her beer spilled down the front of his jeans. "Oh, shit. I'm sorry, Dilly."

He gave her a shrug. "Hell, it's fine, sweetheart. Besides, you outta be drinkin' my beer. Cooper know you're in town?" he asked, looking around the crowd as if in search of him.

Following his lead, she scanned the exuberant bodies packed tight around them, nerves clustering in her stomach. "Yeah, he knows I'm here."

"Asshole." He locked his arm around her neck, pulling her alongside him as he clomped down the road toward the lawn. "I see him every day at the garage. I can't believe he didn't tell me my favorite ginger was home."

"Yeah, you know a lot of redheads?" she quipped, nudging him with her elbow.

His lips split into a lop-sided grin, a dimple denting his rosy cheeks. "None as pretty as you, sweetheart."

She rolled her eyes and returned the smile. It was nice to know that some things hadn't changed. Dilly was still as uncouthly flirtatious as he'd been when he was the Glenley Gator's star lineman in high school.

Weaving them through a long line for an apparent popular beer, Dilly maneuvered her toward the front. Time slowed as her gaze immediately fell on Cooper. He was standing behind the booth, his stance confident and power-ful, his expression carefree and light. Her mouth went dry, and she dug in her heels, stopping Dilly short.

Cooper's strong arms expanded over the sleeves of his black T-shirt, his muscles flexing with every move, sending pulsing shivers through her body. She took a subtle breath and braced herself as she allowed her gaze to travel to his face. A few days' stubble coursed his sharp jaw, and she itched to reach out and brush her fingertips across it, to run her lips over his chin.

Fatigue hung beneath his eyes, but it didn't mar the calm settling in them. His sandy hair curled up around the ears of his backward, fitted baseball hat.

Her stomach plummeted; he was so damn sexy.

"You okay, Halle?" Dilly asked, worry pressing his lips together.

Blinking Dillon into focus, she shouldered aside all the thoughts navigating the maze in her mind and smiled. "Yeah, I'm fine."

He snaked his hand around her waist and said, "Okay,

then. Let's get you another beer."

As they bypassed the excessive line, she gave herself a mental pep talk. She could do this.

"Look what the cat dragged back to town," Dilly announced when they approached the booth. His tone was full of excitement, as if he'd found some long lost treasure. And she held on to that, reminding herself that, even though the rest of the town might not like her here, these other big lugs didn't seem to feel the same way.

"Hey, Hal," Abel greeted, his handsome smile taking over his face as he walked around the booth, sidestepped a couple kegs, then wrapped her in a hug.

She dragged her gaze to the side, just in time to see Cooper's eyes find hers.

Chapter Sixteen

"Here," Abel said, towing his barstool over next to Halle. "Sit. You want a beer?"

Cooper was in the middle of handing a cup of beer to a guy when he felt Halle's eyes on his body. He looked at her and smiled.

"Sure, thanks," she replied to Abel, yet her eyes never once drifted from his.

"Thanks man," Cooper said, dumping the guy's money into the cash box before turning to Halle.

As soon as he was in front of her, he pulled her up off the seat and into his arms, and kissed her forehead. "I was wondering if you were going to come after I told you not to," he teased. He might've been worried about his resolve to keep his distance yesterday, but he had free reign of this woman now, and he was happy as hell she was here.

She smiled up at him but stiffened against his hold. "I'm worried I shouldn't have," she whispered.

His eyes slanted, and he frowned when she placed her palms on his chest and pushed away from him. It might've been a subtle movement, but he'd felt it. "What's wrong?"

"Nothing," she blurted out, shaking her head. "I'm just worried about what people will say if they see us together. If they see *me* with *you* after…"

His teeth threatened to crack beneath the force of his jaw as his muscles clenched tight. "Who gives a fuck what they say."

"*I* do. And I'm afraid you will, too."

He dropped his arms to his sides, aware that his buddies had taken up interest in his and Halle's quiet conversation. "So what is it you want from me, Hal?" he whispered.

"Distance."

"Are you fucking kidding me?"

Panicking, she grabbed his arm. "Just for now. Only here." She swallowed. "I just need to—"

The only thing he wanted to do was pull her back to him and tell her to hell with everyone else. But the past was showing its ugly face to her, and he of all people knew how terrifying that could be. So he nodded. "Only here."

"Thank you."

"But understand one thing, Halle. You *will* be coming home with me. And once I have you in my bed, distance won't exist."

Her tongue darted out and she licked her lips, her green eyes blurring with lust. Unable to resist, he skimmed the back of his knuckles down the side of her arm, reveling in the way she seemed to absentmindedly move toward him.

"Coop? You want another beer?" Abel asked.

Blinking, he stepped away from Halle and shook his

head. "Nah, I'm good."

Dilly laughed. "What? You've only had a couple, don't puss out on us now."

He flipped Dilly off and settled back on his barstool. "I said I'm good."

The beer festival always brought out the entire drinking age population of town, plus those of the surrounding towns as well. Which meant that it was always packed, and tonight was no exception. But he wouldn't be enjoying good beer with his buddies this year. Letting loose around Halle wasn't an option. He already lacked inhibition around her. Alcohol would just add fuel to the fire.

He didn't know how much time had passed as he sat there with his arms folded across his chest, leaning his side against the table while Halle's laughter rang around him. The sound taunted him until his cock stiffened and his skin crawled. Being so damn close to her yet so far away was torture.

The light breeze blew errant curls of hair across her face. God, he could smell her sweet scent from here. Apparently, the universe didn't think being near her was punishment enough, it had to claim all his senses.

"Ha! You deserved that, Dilly!" Halle laughed, and he could no longer keep from looking at her.

Her body was bent forward in silent laughter, her wry curls veiling her face. What he wouldn't give to see her lift her head and direct those green eyes at him while she sang that beautiful laugh.

Abel handed her another beer, and she took a sip, the froth bubbling on her top lip. He had half a fucking mind to yank her ass off that barstool and onto his lap so he could suck the fizz from her lips; so he could show her just how insane she was driving him.

Distracted by Halle, Cooper was halfheartedly paying attention to the people coming and going from the booth. It was likely he would've watched her all night if someone hadn't called out his name.

"Hey, Coop."

Irritated that he had to look away from Halle, he bit down a groan and smiled at the tall brunette who was fiddling in her bag. "Hi, Kara, good to see you," he deadpanned.

She grinned and her carnivorous eyes tore over him. "Yeah? It's been too long. How have you been?" she asked, feigning an innocence he knew all too well was misleading.

The laughter and chatter persisted between his buddies as they continued to hand out beers to the steady line of people in front of their booth, but he didn't fail to notice the one sweet sound that was missing.

He didn't need to look her way to know Halle was watching him, or that her body was wrung tight. He was so acutely aware of that woman he'd know if the steady rhythm of her breathing wavered.

But he looked at her anyway.

He had to.

She was chewing on her bottom lip, her eyes hazy as a result of her empty cup, and as she watched him, he noticed her fingers twisting the fabric of her dress, her foot bouncing from her crossed legs.

Kara cleared her throat, drawing his attention away from Halle.

"Here," he said, handing her a beer.

Her suggestive smile waned. "Thanks. Why don't we

catch up soon?" she asked, moving to the side to allow the person behind her to step up to the booth.

Sure he'd slept with Kara a handful of times, but the only woman he was interested in getting naked was Halle.

Not wanting to be a dick, he kept his mouth shut and gave a firm nod, and that seemed to appease her.

"Okay then, talk to you soon."

He had just said his silent "thank you" for dodging that bullet unscathed when he saw Kara's dark hair fling across her face as she whipped her head back around, her eyes widening as they landed on Halle.

Shit.

Kara's insincere smile gave her away before she even opened her mouth to speak. "Halle? Halle Morgan?"

Halle stopped excessively tapping her foot and tipped her head back to look up at Kara. She blinked. "Yeah, that's me."

"You don't remember me do you? Kara Walsh. I was a year below you."

"Yes," she said. "Of course. I remember you. You were in my AP lit class, right? And weren't you on the cheerleading squad—"

"With Peyton? Yeah, that's me."

Cooper's restraint started to crumble as he watched Halle's smile drop.

"Wow, I haven't seen you around here since…. Gosh, it's been what? Ten years?"

The simple question would have been harmless had it come from anyone other than Kara. The intention behind her words was crystal, and it was fucking working. Halle's face had paled, her shoulders hunching forward.

His legs widened and he leaned forward, resting his arms on this thighs. "I'm pretty sure Halle knows how long she's been gone, Kara."

Kara's snide grin fell from her face as she cut her eyes to him, her brows forming lines across her forehead. "I'm just surprised she's here, that's all, Coop." The cloying tone to her voice made his stomach turn. "No one has seen or heard from her since…hell…since Peyton's funeral." Her head flipped toward Halle, even though she still directed her words to Cooper. "Guess I'm just a little taken back seeing her sitting here with *you* of all people. You know, considering…"

Anger boiled hot in his veins, the increased pounding in his chest drowning out the sound of Kara's voice. The muscles beneath his jaw began to tick as Halle flitted her eyes to his.

There wasn't a chance in hell he was going to sit there and watch her take the blame.

• • •

The intensity emitting from Cooper was palpable. Halle watched as his body seemed to grow, widening, hardening — his muscles rippling through his shoulders as his nostrils flared. He hadn't spoken a word, yet his presence coaxed the attention of everyone around them, their stares fixating on the intimidating man in front of her.

She despised the impulse she had to wrap her arms around him, not only to feel him, though she wanted to desperately, but to ease his tension.

"Kara, you need to go," he growled.

"You seriously can't be defending her after everyone knows why she—"

"I don't need a goddamn reminder, just go."

Halle flinched. His words weren't even directed at her, yet she felt tears begin to pool in her eyes. She'd never been much of a crier, especially not in front of people, but apparently, Cooper was her one exception.

At her dad's funeral, she'd remained stolid. It wasn't until she'd been back at Peyton's house, cradled in Cooper's arms, that she'd finally broken down. He'd stayed with her for hours, comforting her as he mumbled random nothings to her until she cried herself to sleep.

She hadn't cried when she'd found out Peyton had died. Shock had left her a mere shell until Cooper's words brought her back. It'd always been Cooper.

She was afraid this would happen. She *knew* this would happen—that he would react this way. But still, hearing him come to her rescue when he was so obviously hurting…

"Halle, you okay?"

She was staring ahead at the cluster of people in line when she heard Cooper's voice break through her trance. There was no way she could look at him right now, so instead, she forced a smile on her face and stood up.

She needed to regain her composure, stat.

"Hey boys," she said. "I'm going on the hunt for kettle corn. Can I get you anything?"

"I'm good, sweetheart," Dilly said, giving her a pitiful set of puppy dog eyes that told her they weren't buying into her excuse. Not that she expected them to.

Cooper stood and took a single step toward her. "Halle."

She cleared her throat and ignored him. "All right," she

said, her voice cracking. "But I'm not sharing."

Navigating as quickly as she could through the crammed lines at the beer booths, Halle rushed toward the lawn of the square. She needed to find some air that wasn't occupied by drunken bodies.

Her legs quickened the pace as the end of the brick road neared. It was so close, yet so far away. Finally, she stepped onto the grass, her lungs never so grateful to take a deep breath. The breeze picked up her hair, and she sighed as the air tugged at the wispy strands that clung to her sticky neck.

She watched the band switch sets, the lead singer taking a seat on a barstool with his guitar resting on his lap. A few couples gathered around the stage, tangling in each other's arms as they swayed to the slow, strumming tempo.

Inhaling another staggering breath, she wiped beneath her eyes. She was an idiot to think she could handle facing people like Kara. This was Glenley. Secrets didn't exist in this small town. And small towns never forgot.

Everyone knew that she and Peyton had been fighting the night of the accident. They'd never fought, not like that, and with teenage eavesdroppers, it was no surprise that it'd become the talk of the party.

They'd both been drinking, celebrating their graduation—their future—and all she'd been capable of thinking about was Cooper. Butterflies had danced in her stomach every time his gorgeous face had flashed behind her eyes. Tingles had shot straight through her body whenever she'd moved just the right way, arousing the delicious, sore throb between her thighs.

It was never something she'd planned to keep from Peyton—never. She told her everything. She guessed part of her had worried how Peyton would react about her feelings toward Cooper, about sleeping with him.

Turned out she'd been devastated.

She pressed her lips together and shook away the memory. God, she wished she could go back to that night, start it all over again. Change everything.

Save Peyton.

The guilt she'd worked so hard to submerge resettled on the surface. It thickened in her throat and tightened in her chest. It was like the oxygen had been sucked from the air.

Then fingers circled around her wrist, pulling her around and pressing her against a warm, comforting chest. And she could breathe.

Strong, protective arms cradled her tightly, and even as her heart dropped to her stomach, the rest of her relaxed.

Cooper was here.

His gaze gripped her and became the very force keeping her upright. It felt as if time stood still, as if the world had stopped spinning and all that was left was him.

But it didn't take long for the world to right itself. Time moved forward, and her dome of safety burst.

She felt the weight of everyone's stare gravitate toward them. The least they could've done was try to be discrete as they whispered.

But their favorite hometown guy was embracing the woman who'd killed his sister.

They saw the Notre Dame scholar who'd left behind his dream in order to take care of his mother, the man who lived and worked and supported this town. And they saw him comforting the teenager who'd led her best friend to her death, the woman who hadn't been back for ten years.

Cooper was still while he held her, his blue eyes reflecting the light from the strung lanterns overhead. She wanted to burrow her face in his neck and breathe him in. And she would've, if she was capable of looking away from him.

He tipped his head down. "Don't let them see you cry." There it was, the throaty gruff to his voice that always appeared when he softened his words. And she loved it.

Blinking back her tears, she followed him as he dragged her out to the middle of the square, surrounding them with the very people who were staring. He pulled her back into his arms and held her tight. Then he began swaying her side to side, and she completely and helplessly melted into him.

He gathered her close, tracing lazy circles over the dip in her spine, right between the twin dimples above her bottom. She dropped her head to his shoulder. This tender side was too much.

"Hey." He captured her chin between his fingers and forced her to look at him. "Don't worry about them. You hear me?" His palm flattened above her bottom, and he pushed her to him until their hips nestled tightly together.

Words escaped her, and all she could do was stare at him.

He lowered his forehead to hers. "Whatever you've got going on in your head, you're wrong. And so are they. Right now, pretend it's just you and me."

She managed a nod, and his thumb lifted to her lip, tugging it from her teeth before he smoothed his finger across it.

The acoustic melody sounded through the square as they continued to rock against each other, arms tangled, breath coinciding, heartbeats syncing.

Her entire body came alive, tenderly aware of every sweep, every caress… everything. His hand on her back, the way his fingertips continued to find small places on her face to explore: the apples of her cheeks, the crease between her eyes, the bow of her lips.

But eventually, the song ended. She'd cash in all her lucky pennies if she could just rewind the last few minutes.

People started moving along the square again, some twirling and dancing to the new song. But they remained standing where they were, still holding onto each other. She couldn't bring herself to look away from him; she wasn't ready for the moment to end.

"I told you," she whispered.

He pressed her in closer to him, almost as if he was trying to pause, then rewind time as well. Pins prickled her skin as his steel warmth settled against her. "Told me what?"

She smiled weakly. "That the old Cooper I knew was still in there somewhere."

She felt his body tense around her. "What makes you so sure?"

"Because I just found him."

The muscles along his jaw ticked as he tipped his head back to the sky and exhaled. "Fuck."

She didn't know what to say, or what to do. So she snuggled into him. And when he tightened his arms around her, she sighed. *This*. She would never get used to what his touch did to her, the way she craved him in every sense of the word. In every way a woman could crave a man.

Looking up at him, she said, "You were here for me when I needed you. Just like you always used to be."

"Except I *wasn't* always there for you when you needed

me, Hal."

Her shoulders slumped. "Coop…"

Eyes gripping her, he lowered his forehead to hers. "Shh. Not right now, not yet."

Her heart squeezed, blood rushing though her veins as her pulse quickened. She didn't know what he meant, but she heard the truth in his words, like a promise he was afraid to make, but one he'd undoubtedly keep.

A moment passed between them as he clung to her, as if he dreaded letting her go, and her skin prickled beneath his touch.

Standing in the middle of the square, surrounded by people, Halle lost her heart to Cooper Bale all over again.

He lifted his lips and placed a long kiss to her forehead. "Come on."

She followed him back to the booth and watched him pull his keys out of his pocket.

"Hey man," Cooper said, clamping his hand down on Abel's shoulder. "I'm heading out."

Abel frowned. "All right. You good?"

Cooper didn't respond, he just shifted his gaze to her for a single heartbeat before squeezing Abel's shoulder.

Her stomach clenched. She knew that look. It'd been burned in her memory for ten long years. He was about to walk away from her. "Don't. Not again."

His shoulders crumpled, then he turned his hat around and pulled the bill down over his eyes. A defeated groan tore from his throat.

Not caring the least about who could hear or what direction they'd spin this, she stepped in front of him. It didn't matter anymore. "Look at me," she pleaded.

His fingers slipped through her hair, and he crushed her against him. "I'm not that man anymore, Halle. I just need to clear my head. Sort through some shit."

"Okay," she said, trying like hell to hold it together.

He placed a long, hard kiss to her forehead, then turned and left.

Dilly slid up beside her, threw his arm around her shoulders, and hugged her from the side. "Can I get you another beer, sweetheart?"

She shook her head. She needed something a hell of a lot stronger than beer.

Chapter Seventeen

Cooper watched the yellow lines dash past him in a blur as the night stretched out before him. He'd been riding since he left the festival. It felt like only minutes had passed, but several hours had gone by. He didn't have a destination, just needed the quiet to shush his inner battle, needed the purr of the engine to numb his body.

When he'd held Halle in his arms in the middle of the square, it'd felt so damn good, so right. But she'd always felt right.

She'd said she saw the old Cooper, and hell, for a moment, he'd thought that maybe she had—that maybe he could be that man again. For her.

Except that man had died ten years ago alongside Peyton. And the man he was now wasn't enough, not for Halle.

After turning his bike down old Highway 32, he rolled back the throttle. The next five miles were nothing but a smooth stretch of pavement nestled between fields lined with new rows of green cornstalks. So he gunned it, letting the engine roar and the wind beat against his body.

As the fields merged into scattered houses, he slowed his motorcycle and started to drive out of Fayette. Then he saw Halle's car. It sat parked in the same spot as the first night he'd found her at this shit-hole bar.

His temper detonated inside him. What the hell was she doing here? This bar wasn't a place a woman should be at alone. Its customers ranged from the town's low life drunk to the occasional motorcycle club member looking for cold beer and a cheap lay while passing through. That didn't leave much in the way of reliable company.

Without hesitation, he pulled into the lot and parked next to Halle's car. It didn't take but a few seconds for him to tear through the front door.

He spotted her immediately, her red hair and blue dress sticking out among everyone around her. She was leaning her body against the bar for support while she flung her hand out in front of her and laughed, talking to that same asshole from before.

He stalked toward her, bristling as he readied himself for a tantrum. There was no doubt she'd be pissed that he planned on dragging her ass out of this bar again, but he didn't give a shit. He paused behind her while he waited for her to stop rambling. In the meantime, he bored his eyes into the guy sitting next to her.

The asshole grinned at him, like he was accepting some unspoken challenge. Great, all he needed was for this jackass to play like he had some claim over her. He wasn't in the fucking mood.

Cooper stepped closer to her until her shoulder brushed

his stomach. "Halle."

Clumsily, she turned around on her stool, and the look that flashed across her face shocked the ever-loving-hell out of him. "Cooper!"

He was pissed, no doubt about it, but it was difficult to stay mad at her when she was beaming and leaning into him.

Picking up her glass she drained its contents. "What're you doin' here?"

The guy next to her slid his gaze up to Cooper's as Halle relaxed against him, clearly pissed that Cooper once again had intervened and screwed up his plans.

Yeah, that's right fucker.

He skimmed his hand between her shoulder blades; he couldn't help it. Her dress scooped low, her spine just summoning his fingers to trace it. "I'm here to take you home. Come on," he coaxed, hoping to prevent a repeat reaction of the last time.

"Mmph, hold on." She raised her hand and wiggled her fingers at the bartender. "Can I get another?" she asked, tapping her finger on her empty glass. "And a beer for him." She nodded toward Cooper.

"Nah, I'm good."

"Come on, Coop. Have a drink with me," she begged, leaning into him a little more.

"I don't think you need another drink, babe. Let's go."

Giggling, she smiled up at him, and he found himself staring at the way the corners of her eyes creased. Then she groaned and dropped her head against his side. "Hold on." Her fingers clutched his thigh, and her eyes squeezed shut. "I'm...spinning."

She was trashed. He felt the whip of frustration start

to thrash in his muscles. Why was she being so careless? If he'd not shown up tonight, what would she have done? Fire gripped the nape of his neck, burning a path down his spine at the thought of that fucker trying to take her home. Or her getting behind the wheel...

Straightening, he blinked and pushed away the nightmare. He was here, so there was no chance in hell either of those would happen.

"Okay," she grunted. "I think...they've...stopped." She leaned up, impishly smiling. "And you were right, I definitely...don't need another."

He pulled a fifty out of his wallet and put it under her empty glass. "Come on, lush," he said, grabbing her purse and wrapping his arm around her waist.

Her eyes squinted, and she snickered at him. "Are you teasing me, Cooper Bale?"

He easily lifted her off the stool and placed her feet on the floor, keeping his arm around her as he tested her balance. He laughed. "Just calling it how I see it. Let's get you home."

Her eyes widened and she staggered, his arms the only thing keeping her off the grimy floor. "But my cab isn't here yet." She panicked, trying to regain her footing.

Thank God. Small rolls of reassurance kneaded the knots in his muscles. "You called a cab?"

"Yeah," she mumbled, looking at the watch on her wrist, squinting in a futile attempt to read the time. Huffing, she dropped her arm. "They should be here soon." Her words mushed together incoherently.

"I'm taking you home, babe."

She smiled up at him as he led her out the door, her hazy

eyes rousing with lust.

When they reached her car, he dug in her purse and retrieved her keys before helping her inside and buckling her in. She let her head fall back onto the headrest and sighed as her lids rolled shut.

He assumed she'd fallen asleep when he started the car and she didn't stir, but just as he pulled onto the road, she whispered, "Thank you."

Looking over at her, his heart tightened, shifting in his chest as if gravitating toward her. "I told you —I've got you."

"But you…walked away from me again." Stray curls fell across her face, and as he swiped them away, she leaned into his touch, her body reclining to the side until she was snuggled as close to him as the seats would allow.

"Yeah." What else was he supposed to say? She was fucking right. He did.

She rested her head on his shoulder. "I loved you so much." Then she yawned and burrowed in to him.

His head jerked toward her and his hands tightened on the steering wheel. God, he didn't want to do this, not right now, not when she was drunk.

"Even before I loved you, I loved you," she mumbled, and his stomach flipped.

"I know," he whispered, lifting his arm and wrapping it around her. He knew exactly what she meant. He'd loved her long before he fell in love with her, too. He'd always loved her.

She nuzzled contentedly into the crook of his shoulder and sighed. She was in his arms, relying on the safety of his touch, her trust, her love, her warmth, all seeping into his soul.

Moaning, she rubbed her cheek against his shirt, situating herself as she dawdled on the realm of drunken sleep. "I still love you," she whispered.

He couldn't tell if this was agony, or bliss, didn't know where one stopped and the other one started. Because she made him feel it all.

Only she loved the idea of the man he once was. It didn't matter if he forgave himself and faced the fucking past like she wanted him to. When it came down to it, if she knew the truth about what had happened the night Peyton died, Halle would never look at him the same way again.

Chapter Eighteen

Halle tried to swallow, but her mouth was dry, the residual coating of olives and vodka turning her stomach. She'd drunk too much. Way too much.

"Uhh," she groaned and rolled over.

Slowly, she sat up and assessed the bare room around her. The blanket covering her was an old throw quilt, and the sheet and pillow dressing the bed were mismatched. The only furniture in the room apart from the bed she was in was a small nightstand to the side of her. And even though she'd never stepped foot in this room before, she knew exactly where she was. She could smell Cooper all around her.

Two pills and a glass of water sat next to a lone picture fame on the nightstand. Oh thank God. After popping the Advil in her mouth, she gulped the water, disappointed that it did little to quench her thirst.

A little too quick, considering her head was still swimming, she climbed out of bed. She hissed in a breath as her bare feet hit the cold hardwood floor. She vaguely remembered Cooper coming to the bar, and though she couldn't recall the ride home, she knew he'd driven her. But had he carried her in here? Had he undressed her?

Frowning, she pulled on the white T-shirt that was draping her body. Of course he had. It was Cooper. She looked back at him. His arm was tossed across his eyes, his bare chest expanding from his heavy breaths. He was so sexy.

The hinges creaked as she pulled the door open enough to squeeze out into the hallway. She hated the idea of walking around Cooper's house, alone, at night, and in the dark. It felt sneaky, like she was invading his privacy. But her mouth still felt like the Sahara. Tiptoeing, she made her way in the direction she hoped would lead her to the kitchen.

When she rounded the corner, she stepped into the living room. Only there was nothing about this space that reflected anyone actually lived here. A leather couch sat at the back of the room, directly across from a large LCD TV that hung on the opposite wall. That was it. Not a single table, or lamp, or chair. Nothing. The walls were bare, the windows were undressed, and the entire room felt cold—unlived in.

Guilt slapped her across the face with a cold sting that numbed her entire body. This man carried it all. The guilt of his sister's death, the blame and the responsibility for his mother's depression. God, he gave up everything. Everything. And all he had to show for his sacrifice was a broken heart and a lonely existence. It wasn't the life he'd wanted; it wasn't the life she'd wanted for him.

Suddenly, nothing else mattered but going to him.

She shuffled back down the hall and stopped in front of his door. After a few hesitant moments, she pushed it open and stepped inside.

Deep ridges and valleys of muscle landscaped the man before her. His chest rose and fell in long exaggerated breaths, contrary to her gulping pants. Hung low beneath the sharp cut of his hips was a thin white sheet, tangled between his massive thighs, his bare feet sticking out from beneath it.

The width of his shoulders spanned wide as his arm dangled over the side of the bed and wavy tufts of hair tousled over his forehead, brushing the tops of his eyes.

Exhaustion lined his mouth, and worry gently bunched between his sleeping eyes. He was in absolute need of a haircut, a shave, and a full eight hours sleep—but even then he was the most beautiful creature she'd ever laid eyes on.

She felt like the brave girl who'd snuck into his room ten years ago. Fearless of the power he had over her—the power his body claimed from her.

She held her breath and took a single step. But the moment Cooper's eyes blinked open, she froze.

She watched as he inhaled a deep breath, like her presence was a balm to an ache he couldn't reach. And she went weak.

"Hey," he whispered, his voice raspy from sleep. "Come here." He lifted his arm, opening up his embrace for her to fall into.

A tight burn scaled her throat and her heart pounded. Déjà vu entered her like a vivid dream replaying before her very eyes.

She went to him, her body so completely drawn to him, her emotions so raw, that falling into his arms felt like the only viable way she could breathe.

His eyes raked over her in penetrating sweeps, and when

she reached the edge of the bed, he tugged her into his arms. He laughed softly. "I was dreaming about you."

"Were you?" Her body seeped into him as he obliterated any possible space between them.

"Every night since I'd first had you." He tightened his arm around her. "Feels good to finally have you pressed up beside me when I wake."

"I'm sorry," she whispered against his chest.

"You don't ever have to be sorry for waking me up."

She was glad for the smile that crept on her face, but she shook her head. "That's not what I meant."

His hand skated beneath her T-shirt, and his fingertips brushed up and down her back. "Don't. Just let me have this. Let me have you," he murmured into her hair and pressed a light kiss to her temple. "Just like this, baby," he begged. "Just one last time."

She felt her heart crumple, but she nodded and nuzzled his neck until her lips were just below his jaw. "I don't want it to be the last time," she whispered.

Groaning, he gathered her closer, the strength of his arms crushing her as he rolled to his back, pulling her until half of her body was sprawled on top of him.

They stayed like that for a ceaseless amount of moments, his hand rubbing her back, and his fingers stroking her hair. Her skin was sensitive, his calloused fingers so tender that even the faintest of touches detonated tingles that shot throughout her entire body.

His lips dusted a single kiss to the corner of her eye. It was so simple, so brief, but the intimacy in that one kiss drew a sigh from her mouth. As she burrowed into the comfort of his body, her thigh brushed between his, and her center rocked against his hip.

"Halle," he moaned. "Wait."

"I don't want to wait," she said.

"We really need to talk. There're things I have to tell you." He swallowed. "Things you won't want to hear."

She pushed him onto his back, then rose to her knees and pulled the T-shirt over her head.

"I don't want to talk," she said. "I want you to make love to me."

He started to speak, but she pressed her mouth to his, afraid she already knew what he was going to say. Their tongues found each other, and she felt his resolve disappear. With a groan, he broke their kiss, gripped her hips, and buried his head on her belly, sighing as he pulled her closer to him. The tufts of his messy hair tickled her skin as she combed her fingers through the tangles and massaged his scalp.

His muscled arms wrapped around her waist, pinning her hips to his chest. His desperation filled an ache in her soul she wasn't aware existed until she felt it mend. "You're a good man," she murmured as she stroked his hair. His arms flexed around her, and he tipped his head to the side, maneuvering his lips to the flare of her hip. Tingles danced across her flesh from his tender kiss, liquid heat accumulating between her thighs.

"I wish I was. I told you I don't know how to feel the good without the bad." He kissed her again, except this time he pushed down the thin strap of her thong, loving her with his mouth as he kissed her lower on her hips. "I'm not the man I used to be."

"Cooper…shut up."

She pressed his head into her legs. The flat of his tongue

lapped at the top of her thigh, and she lost the ability to form coherent thoughts. He trailed his open mouth to her other hip, tending to it with the same, leisure attention.

"Yes," she pleaded, digging her nails into his scalp as his teeth nipped the inside of her thigh.

He moaned his approval and ran his mouth over the narrow lace covering her sex. The wet heat of his tongue seeped through her panties, and her body froze as he inhaled deeply. "I could get off by the smell of your arousal alone."

Oh god.

"So sweet…" He yanked her panties to her knees. "And the way you taste on my tongue drives me insane."

Her head fell back as he licked between her drenched folds, ever so slowly swirling the tip on her sensitive clit.

Already, pleasure welled inside her, releasing breathless moans that begged for more of the slow torture, while craving immediate relief. She felt as if she was starting and stopping and reversing all while propelling toward the kind of ecstasy she'd never experienced before.

Two long fingers aided his mouth, plunging deep inside her. And she thought she was going to collapse, her legs no longer able to keep her upright as tremors of pleasure began to spread.

"Cooper, I can't…"

"I've got you," he promised.

She trusted him. So she let her body go, let her muscles turn weak. And she let the pleasure tear straight through her.

"Cooper!" she cried, throwing her head back as she slumped in his arms.

A quiet chuckle pierced the colorful haze swirling behind her eyelids. "You still with me, baby?"

Moaning, her eyes fluttered open. She lay on her back, on the bed, with Cooper now leaning over her. She hadn't even felt him move her. "I think so?"

He smiled, the same smile she'd seen the first time he made love to her all those years ago. Brushing his lips across her skin, he whispered, "Good."

• • •

The feeling of Halle coming undone against his face continued to rumble through Cooper. He loved the way her skin flushed pink, the way her legs quivered, and the way the muscles of her stomach tightened. Watching this woman come was sexy.

"I'm not quite sure what you did to me." She blushed, stretching her body beneath him.

"I am. And I plan to do it again. But first, I need to kiss you. I need your hands on my neck," he said as he grabbed her wrists, placing her hands on the back of his neck, "and your legs around my waist." He dragged his hands down the outsides of her thighs, enjoying the way her eyes drifted shut for a brief moment, then lifted her legs and crossed them behind his back.

"Yeah? What else?" she said.

And goddamn, if he hadn't already known that this woman had a death grip on his damaged heart, then he would have in that very moment. Looking at her soft and compliant against him, her body tangled with his, giving him what he needed simply because he needed her to—he had no words.

Halle Morgan.

"That's it, babe. The only other thing I need you to do is kiss me."

She smiled. "I think I can do that."

Then their lips met, and the entire world slipped away. It was just her. The taste of her tongue, the pressure of her goddamn perfect lips. The way her fingers prodded the back of his neck, twirling the hair at his nape. The way the insides of her thighs squeezed his hips as she writhed around in even measure with the thrashing of their tongues.

Her legs dropped from around his waist, and just as he was about to protest, she pushed his boxers down with her toes.

A deep rasp ripped from his throat when his cock met the warmth of her center, her pussy cradling him as she rubbed against him. "You know what I need?" she murmured against his lips, still driving him mad with the way she rolled her hips beneath him. "I *really* need you inside me."

Holding her gaze, he drew his hips back, then sank inside her.

There was no possibility of ever getting used to the way her pussy clung to his cock while he worked in and out, tenaciously rubbing against her clit. It'd never been this good.

He stilled inside her, pressure building at the base of his spine when her tight pussy drew him in deeper.

"Cooper"—she circled her hips, knocking on his resolve—"don't stop. I need you."

The words should have healed him, but now, they only reminded him of what he would lose when this moment ended and he told her what he should've said as soon as she stepped into his room.

He wrapped his arm around her and rolled them over,

pulling her on top of him. As she settled onto her knees astride him, he palmed her ass, his fingers spreading her open while he repositioned her above him. One thrust of his hips and he was inside her. *God, yes.*

At least he could give her one final memory of them together before he lost her forever.

He splayed his hands on the side of her neck, trailing them down to her collarbone. "I've never seen anything so damn beautiful."

A blush fanned her cheekbones as she bit down on her bottom lip, then rolled her hips forward.

"Fuuck," he murmured. The sight of her riding his cock drew his balls tight. "Put your hands on my shoulders."

Her hands came down and rested on him, putting her breasts in line with his mouth, just where he wanted them. Once he had her nipple between his lips, he sucked and pulled and nibbled until her fingernails dug into the pads of his shoulders.

Her rhythm turned merciless. "Oh God. Cooper. I'm so close…I…Uhnn."

It was all so good—the way her moans coincided with his panting, the way she ground herself against him, his name on her lips.

Pinning his hips to the mattress, he grabbed ahold of her waist, stilling her above him, and then he thrust up into her. She cried out.

So he did it again.

And again.

"Oh please," she begged, trying desperately to move beneath his hold, to seek out that last little bit of friction she needed to send her flying.

He brushed a hand up between her shoulders, brought her chest down to his, and kissed her. He imbibed her moans as he devoured her mouth, claiming every part of her he possibly could in that moment as he thrust up into her, one, two, three times, the new angle of her body causing him to hit just where she needed it...

He felt her breath stagger and her body tighten. "Cooper, I'm—"

"Right there with you, baby. Give it to me." Gripping her hip, he rolled her down on top of him the same time he thrust hard and quick. Her head reared back and her body bucked as she moaned through the most beautiful fucking orgasm he'd ever watched cross her face.

Slamming into her one last time, he met his release, his vision blurring as she tightened around his cock, her body milking him for every drop he had.

He held her like that until her shudders lessened to tiny little quakes, until her pussy relaxed.

Then he held her longer, wishing time to slow so the moment wouldn't end.

Fuck.

He was a prick to think he could be with her. She deserved better than him—better than a man who let her down time and time again, a man who couldn't face his own goddamn memories. But he'd never been able to resist her. When he told her the truth, maybe this time she'd have better luck staying away from him.

Chapter Nineteen

Lazy warmth blanketed Halle, coaxing her to wake. And when she did, she was greeted by Cooper's large body wrapped behind her.

Carefully so as not to wake him, she lifted his heavy arm from around her waist and scooted out from under him. She took a moment to stretch her body, curling her toes and arching her back as she quietly yawned. She was deliciously sore, aching and throbbing in all the right places, courtesy of their night together.

After quickly sliding on her panties and Cooper's T-shirt, Halle crept out of his room, tiptoeing to the guest room for her purse. It was only seven thirty in the morning. She wasn't sure how long Cooper liked to sleep in, but she figured she had some time to at least cook some breakfast.

Except when she got to the kitchen, cabinet after cabinet was empty. And when she'd poked around in his fridge, she'd been severely disappointed. She might be one hell of a cook, but even she couldn't whip something up in this kitchen. Not unless the main ingredients were beer and left over pizza.

With her head taking the brunt of her alcohol binge from last night, Halle finally settled on a cup of instant coffee, and a couple Aspirin. It was inevitable, she and Coop needed to talk. About yesterday, last night, hell, the last two weeks. Everything. But, she'd take the blame for last night. That was on her.

Faint pulses vibrated between her thighs as she allowed her mind to replay the night before. She wasn't quite sure how long she sat at the kitchen table before she heard Cooper's bedroom door creak and the muted thud of his feet coming down the hall.

"Morning," he said from behind her.

She glanced over her shoulder and smiled. "Morning. You want some coffee?"

He moved up next to her and sat down. "No, thanks, though."

All of a sudden, the contents of her mug became increasingly interesting. Or she could call it like it was—fear. She was afraid whatever words were about to be shared between them would shatter what little piece of them they had intact.

"Hey…"

When she lifted her eyes to look at him, her throat constricted. The pounding of her head had nothing on her heart.

"We need to talk."

She nodded. "I know." It took a moment to gain the courage, because she didn't know how he would respond, but she finally pulled a picture out of her purse and slid it in front of him. "But before we do, I wanted to give you this."

The muscles of his jaw clenched tight as he gazed down at the image of him, Halle, and Peyton, the Halloween photo from the memory box.

He cleared his throat, but it didn't do much to hide the strain in his word. "Why?"

She took a deep breath and released it. "Because you need to face the past, Coop."

Briefly, he looked over at her, but she couldn't decipher the emotion in his eyes before he shook his head and glanced back down at the photo. "And what if I can't? What if I can't face the fact that my baby sister called me moments before she died—and I missed it?"

Ice slithered across her skin. "What are you talking about?"

"I'm talking about the voicemail Peyton left me the night she died."

The coffee burned her tongue, scalding her throat, as she took a gulp to try and dislodge the lump that had formed. "I didn't know she left you a message."

"I didn't, either, not until I heard it while I was sitting in your hospital room, waiting for you to wake up. But it was too late."

Her hand flew to her mouth, and she shook her head. "What did it say?"

He hesitated, taking a breath and releasing it while she waited patiently for him to tell her.

"Fuck, I've listened to that message over a hundred times," he said, dropping his elbows to the table, resting his head on his hands. "She was worried I would break your heart, warned me not to. She couldn't stand the thought of you being hurt." He finally said, "Then she begged me to answer the phone, said she needed me to come pick you both up." He looked up at Halle. "Then I heard her yell into the distance, asking you not to leave without her."

"You know that doesn't make it your fault, Coop."

He shut his eyes and exhaled. "Like hell it doesn't," he bit out.

Halle's body convulsed as her tears came hard and fast, her sobs raking through her body with a force that broke his damn heart all over again.

In an instant, Cooper had pulled her onto his lap and wrapped his arms around her. With her head buried in his neck, her embrace squeezing the life from his soul, she cried, "God, Coop. And you had to hear all that on your phone knowing that once she got in that car with me... I'm so sorry."

"Dammit, Halle. *I'm sorry.* Don't you fucking get it? If I would've answered when she'd called, she would've never gotten in that car. *You* would've never gotten in that car."

"But I did get in that car. And Peyton followed *me*." She silently counted off the seconds that passed as her hiccupped breath evened, and her body relaxed.

"But you know what?" she said, standing up from his lap. "You're right. The blame *is* on you. You were all I had left, and you let me leave the only home I knew. *You* shut me out, and *you* walked away from me. Just like you've done every time you lowered your guard enough for me to let you back in. All because you can't face the past?"

Anguish tore from his chest. "Dammit. I don't want to hurt you."

Frowning, she grabbed her purse off the table. "You already did. And I can't trust that you won't do it again."

Heat seared her eyes as they refilled with tears. She pressed her lip together and slid the picture back in front of him. "They're just memories, Coop," she said, nodding toward the picture. "I didn't want to face them, either. But I learned that the good outweighed the bad. *You* outweighed bad."

She held his gaze for a few more heartbeats, then leaned down and pressed a kiss to his lips. "And it's okay to feel them both."

Then this time, she walked away.

Chapter Twenty

After enduring the last ten years, Cooper hadn't thought it was physically possible for it to hurt worse, but it was. He'd feared Halle would yank him so far back into the past that he wouldn't escape. And he'd been right.

"Mom?" Cooper called out, the front door slamming against the wall as he barreled into the house. His mom had called him, asking him to come over after work. He couldn't remember the last time his mom had called him during the day, asking to see him. Which naturally scared the ever-loving hell out of him.

She'd been doing so well. It'd only been a week since Halle had left, and though his mom appeared to be doing great, he couldn't risk it. The thought that something might be wrong had him out the door and on his way to her house before he'd even hung up the phone.

"I'm in the kitchen," she hollered.

The aroma of orange blossom perfumed the air as he made

his way down the hallway to the kitchen. "Hey, everything okay?" he asked as he stepped up behind her. She was sitting at the table, examining something in front of her.

When she didn't respond, he laid his hand on her shoulder. Her skin was warm on his palm, and it was hard to believe that such a short time ago he would have felt nothing but bone beneath his touch. "Mom," he coaxed.

Peering over her shoulder to get a glance at what held her attention, he felt his stomach bottom out. "Where'd you get that?"

His mom pushed the tin box to the side, giving him a better view of its contents. "It came in the mail this afternoon. From Halle."

Peyton and Halle's memorabilia overflowed from the small box.

Shit.

Clearing his throat, he pushed the box back in front of his mom and sat down in the seat next to her. "She just sent this to you? Did she leave a note or anything?"

Without saying anything, his mom handed him a single sheet of paper, and his fingers shook as he unfolded it. Three lines were penned in Halle's sloppy cursive on the center of the page, and he sucked in a breath as he read the words.

It was so good to see you—to be home.

Thank you for everything.
Love, Halle.

The note said so much in so few words. And he knew— she wouldn't come back this time. The recognizable heat of anger radiated though his chest. If this was the universe's way of handing out some sort of punishment, it was doing one hell of a job.

The day Peyton had died, an irreversible pain had claimed him. And he'd sworn that pain intensified the moment Halle walked back into his life. But now? Just knowing that he would never again feel the relief that only she could give him made the agony intolerable.

He deserved it, though. There were only so many times a woman could watch a man walk away from her before she did the same thing. And that was exactly what had happened. He'd pushed her right out that door.

But he wanted her back.

"Cooper," his mom said, dragging his attention away from the note. "I owe you an apology."

"What?" he stammered. "No, Mom. You have nothing to be sorry for. This"—he lifted the paper out in front of him—"this is my fault."

A sad smile creased her lips. "No, sweetheart. I do have something to be sorry for. But first, I also want you to know how grateful I am to you."

"Mom—"

She shook her head. "I know you put your life on hold to take care of me. You're a good man, Cooper. I wouldn't have made it after Peyton died if I didn't have you. So thank you."

He grabbed her hand and squeezed it tight. He didn't know what to say, so he hoped that said enough.

They stayed silent like that for a few more seconds before his mom lifted her palm to his cheek and smiled. "I'm okay—I'm better. Because of you. And because of Halle."

She lifted the box from the table and placed it in his hands.

"Now, it's your turn," she whispered. "Peyton would want you to be happy. *Both* of you."

He clutched the box in his grip until his knuckles blanched white.

There was only one way he would ever be okay—would ever be *better*. Halle had begged him to face the past. To live with it. Accept it. Learn from it. And finally, to move past it.

He stood from the chair and placed a kiss on his mom's forehead before turning to leave.

"Bring her home," his mom said.

His feet stalled, and he glanced back at her, nodding once.

That was exactly what he had planned to do.

• • •

Halle kicked her shoes off by the front door. Oh, if felt so good to get out of them. She and Courtney had catered a "his and hers" baby shower, and her feet throbbed from standing in heels for the last four hours.

She fished her phone out of her purse to call and order a pizza. The last week had been hard, and she was looking forward to a DVR recap night. Pizza, martinis, and pajamas, what more could she ask for?

Cooper.

"No, don't start that again, Halle," she said, peeling out of her clothes, leaving a trail behind her as she headed to her bedroom.

It'd been exactly seven days since she'd left Glenley, yet she hadn't been able to climb out of the funk she'd been in ever since she'd returned to Columbus. After spending time in the town she grew up in, and with the family she missed more than she'd known, she just couldn't seem to find a way to conquer her sadness.

Leaving Glenley was for the best, though as each day passed, she found herself questioning the reasons why.

Then she remembered. Cooper was why she left. If she'd thought her body had betrayed her, then what did that say about her heart? Because it ached. It felt like every beat only made her miss him more.

Yawning, she pulled her hair out of her ponytail and opened up her pajama drawer. There were only a few things she'd kept for herself before she sent the keepsake box back to Kathryn. She hadn't been able to bring herself to put Cooper's old football T-shirt back in there.

She pulled it out of her drawer, and that persistent pang in her chest vibrated like a ringing bell, echoing how much she missed him. She hated herself for it, because missing him wasn't going to change anything.

But she slipped the T-shirt on anyway.

Once again, she'd been reduced to *that* woman. There'd been a countless number of times she'd had to talk herself out of going to him. Was she crazy for wanting to hear his voice? Because it sure felt like she was going crazy without him. Hell, maybe she was. What kind of a woman would crave a man who'd been the reason for her broken heart all these years? What kind of woman would love a man who'd only proven he would break her heart again and again?

She would—and she did.

But, sometimes, love wasn't enough to chase away the bad, and as Cooper had told her himself, he couldn't have one without the other.

She'd gotten through the last ten years, and she could do it again. She just didn't want to. Not without him.

After wiping the makeup from her face, she ambled into the kitchen. It was a dirty martini kind of night, but she might just skip the olives and go straight to the vodka. Hell, she might even skip the shot glass and go straight to the bottle.

Just as she was getting the vodka from the pantry, the doorbell rang. It was as if her tummy had a sixth sense and rumbled its appreciation for the greatness that is pizza delivery.

Quickly, she grabbed her wallet out of her purse, and kicked her high heels out of the way so she could open the door. "That was fa—"

Her words evaporated. Every nerve in her body tightened, and she felt as if she was in a dream, falling and falling and falling, unable to wake up.

Cooper was here.

"Hey." The deep, familiar gruff of his voice zapped her skin to life by sound alone. But his gaze—it was as if it caressed her, burned along every single inch of her body, drinking her in as if he'd been parched for weeks.

She leaned against the door, silently praying her legs would support her. "Hi," she said, trying her best to sound as unaffected as possible.

He looked like the Cooper she remembered, the Cooper she'd first fallen in love with when she was nothing more than a girl. The broad muscles of his shoulders heaved with a sigh, and he shook his head, a wry grin curving his lips. "You had to be wearing my shirt, didn't you?"

Air lurched into her lungs as he stepped into her, his

body so close to hers, the denim of his jeans rasped against her bare legs.

She felt the heat start at her neck, fanning up to her cheeks. Looking down, she pressed her thighs together. Her body was betraying her just like it had time and time again, sizzling in anticipation for his touch that would inevitably come—she knew it would.

With his hand resting on the doorframe above her head, he bowed over her, his mouth scurrying warm breath along her lips as he tipped his forehead close to hers. "God, Halle. I've missed you so damn much."

His words took their time tumbling through her, and she instinctively pressed her palms against his chest, unsure whether to push him away or pull him in.

When she was confident she could speak without her voice shaking, she asked, "What are you doing here?"

He smiled, and God, she hadn't seen that easy, genuine smile since the morning of her graduation. "I told you—I miss you, babe."

Blinking her eyes closed for a moment, she sighed. "Coop, I miss you, too, but—"

She gasped as the weight of his chest crashed down on her, and speaking became impossible as his lips melded to hers. His hands found their way into her hair, his thumbs resting on her cheeks as he tipped her head back, kissing her deeper.

The ferocity she was so used to him claiming when he kissed her was absent. Instead, his mouth was soft, his lips careful and intimate. But even though the ravaging sweeps of his tongue had been replaced with sexy caresses, it was just as intense. And it liquefied her insides.

"You ruined me, babe," he said against her lips, still working her mouth over with his. "You fuckin' slayed me."

She pulled back. She couldn't go there again. "Cooper—"

"Loving you destroys me. But that's all I want, baby. I love you so goddamn much. You ripped my chest open and took ownership of my broken heart."

Peering up at him, she watched as his eyes transformed, passion and desire swirling. He groaned, the gravely sound reaching her core, and she could feel her body responding to him.

Cooper snaked his arm around her waist in a movement so quick she startled. "I want to show you something," he said, pulling her body to his, then running his hands down her sides, his strong fingers kneading her thighs. "But first, I'm going to need you to put something on these legs."

Suppressing a moan, she stammered, "What? No, you can't just come here and—"

Cooper's hands slip beneath the hem of her T-shirt and cupped her butt, urging her to roll her hips against him. And God, when she did, she wanted to cry out from the feel of his erection pressing hard against her.

"Have it your way," he said, a smooth grin turning up his lips as he tugged her out the door.

"What are you doing?" she shrieked, but his hand never loosened from hers.

She lived on a quiet street, her house sitting back away from the road, but she still had neighbors. Regardless that the sky had turned dark, her butt was barely covered.

But when she noticed what was parked in her driveway, she forgot all about what she was—or wasn't—wearing. "I can't believe you still have this."

His old Ford pickup sat in the driveway. The exterior had been painted a new shade of blue, the years' worth of rust along the bottom no longer there, and the dent in the front bumper where Cooper had taken out a tree while mudding had been fixed.

The passenger door was open, and Cooper was guiding her into the cab before she even finished gawking at it. "Slide in."

She did as he asked, the leather warm on the backs of her thighs as she settled into the seat. It was strange, the feelings that bombarded her. This truck had been a staple of her adolescence, and the memories were countless.

"You're smiling," he said when he climbed behind the wheel and shut the door.

She shrugged. She hadn't realized she was. Who knew she would be sentimental over a vehicle? "I'm just surprised to be sitting in this truck again. I figured you got rid of it."

It was Cooper's turn to shrug. "Too many memories," he said as a sort of explanation, but she understood.

"Yeah. I'm glad you showed me."

"The truck was just an unexpected bonus. This"—he reached behind the seat—"is what I wanted to show you."

She pressed her lips together, her eyes going wide as he rested the memory box on the seat between them. She looked to him in question, a smile her only answer. If he kept this up, she would swear she was sitting next to the same boy she'd fallen in love with.

"Open it."

A million questions hit her at once, but she reluctantly lifted the lid and sat it on the dashboard.

"I thought we could have our own box," he said. "Hold

on to some of the good memories."

Memories? She swallowed hard. Her hands shook as she reached in and pulled out a small Mason jar. "Has Dilly traded brewing beer for distilling moonshine?" she asked, turning the jar over in her hands.

He smiled. "Rain water."

There was a pause, then her heart leaped, and she felt it start to race as she realized the sentiment. Rain—it held a new meaning for her now. Images flashed through her mind of Cooper kissing her outside the bar, the rain blanketing them. Goose bumps flared on her bare legs. Yes, the rain was definitely a good memory.

He grabbed the single picture from the box and held it out for her. Her eyes skimmed the picture, and fourteen-year-old Cooper smiled back at her. "The Halloween picture," she said, taking it from his hands.

"That was a good night. For all of us. And you made a pretty cute zombie."

She laughed. "Thanks. And what's this?" she asked, picking up the large leaf at the bottom.

"It's from the Sycamore, the one by Peyton's grave."

It felt debasing to just acknowledge him with a nod, but that's all she could offer.

"Halle…"

Once the chill worked its way through her veins, she looked at him. "I thought you wanted to hold on to the good memories."

The oxygen in the cab depleted with his large breath, but it didn't make a difference; she couldn't breathe anyway. Sighing, he clasped his fingers around her chin and brought his forehead to hers, his warm breath feathering over her lips. "I've faced the past, baby. I'll take all the pain, endure every ounce of hell it brings our way, so long as I get to have you. You're my future."

"Cooper..."

He set the box on the floorboard, then in the next breath pulled her astride his lap. "I love you, Halle. I've always loved you."

The steel ridges of his muscles etched along her body as his hands flattened on her back, securing her to him. Then his face was buried in the curve of her shoulder, his mouth dragging whimpers from her throat as he kissed her with a tenderness she thought was gone.

"I'm not walking away—not without you. I'm taking you home."

His words, his body, his voice—they were breaking her down bit by bit, and she felt herself helplessly absorbing his body against hers. She missed him...

"Tonight," he said.

Her brows darted up. "What?" she asked, leaning back to look at him.

"Yeah, babe." He smiled—and she melted. "I'm not walking away, and I'm not letting you walk away, either. You're coming home with me."

"Tonight? It takes over three hours to get to Glenley from here."

"No sense of arguing with me, baby. You'll be home... in my bed...with me...tonight." He kissed the hollow at the base of her throat and squeezed her against him. "I'll bring you to get your things tomorrow. I just need you home."

God, she loved this man. And he was here for her—faced his demons for *her*.

She tightened her legs around him, twined her hands at his neck, and kissed the corner of his mouth. "Will we survive this?"

He grinned, a smile that not only made her knees wobble but made her heart melt. "We already did, babe," he said, lowering her down onto the bench seat.

Skimming his hands up her shirt, his fingers tickled her newly sensitive skin. "I think this belongs back in the box." He lifted the shirt over her head, leaving her bare breasts exposed.

"I think you're right."

He soaked up the sight of her as if he had all the time in the word, all the while making her squirm like crazy. "I'm going to make love to you," he whispered, pressing his lips to her throat.

"Right here?"

"Right now, here in my truck."

She smiled at him, remembering when he'd said those same words to her before. Yes, God, yes, she wanted him to make love to her—needed his body inside hers. Biting her bottom lip, she nodded.

Cooper's mouth lowered to her stomach, dotting a path of kisses over her belly button, between the valley of her breasts, and up the center of her throat, before he finally kissed her lips. "I'm going to make you come. Then I'm taking you home where you belong."

Epilogue

Standing out of the way, Cooper settled his shoulder against the wall and watched as Halle turned their kitchen into a five star restaurant. He'd already offered to help her make Thanksgiving dinner twice, but after seeing her organized culinary chaos, he was glad she'd shot him down.

With Halle living with him, his kitchen had seen more action in the last five months than it had in the last five years. The side effect had him picking up a couple of extra hours at the gym every week, but he wasn't complaining.

"Smells good," he said before taking a drink from his beer bottle.

Her hair was pulled back away from her face, giving him a perfect view of her profile as she smiled and peeked into the oven. "I hope so."

"You okay?"

He'd known she was nervous when she woke up before the sunrise to preheat the oven and toss the endless amount of bread crumbs she'd made to make sure they were drying out evenly. But the crack in her voice tipped him off to just how nervous she truly was.

Regardless of the fact that anything would be better than the piss poor attempt he and Abel had made the last few years, her food was always amazing.

But this would be the first Thanksgiving they were together again, not to mention she had to all but threaten his mom in order to talk her into letting Halle do all the cooking, so he could imagine she was feeling the pressure.

"Yeah, of course."

He smiled, already assuming she'd say that. "You cook for a living. You'll be fine, babe," he assured.

"It's Thanksgiving, and I'm making your mom's stuffing recipe," she pointed out, as if to say he didn't know what the hell he was talking about.

"Yes, and I know it'll be great."

She smiled at him, but that smile didn't rival the ones he'd seen her give him since she'd been back. "I just want today to be perfect." She sighed.

"It will be." He walked up behind her and placed a kiss on the back of her neck. The knife in her hand stilled mid-slice as she leaned against him. "Hey," he whispered.

"Hmm," was her only reply—along with the goose bumps that erupted across her skin—before her focus returned to the cutting board.

"Why don't you take a break with me?"

A roar of disappointed profanity sounded from the living room, accompanied by Rilynn's gloating. He hoped like hell the Bears hadn't just scored against the Colts.

Halle's gaze followed the sounds, and she smiled. "As

soon as I get these mushroom caps stuffed. I promised Abe I'd make them. Then I'm all yours...for about twenty-five minutes."

"I can work with that." More chills spread across her skin when he breathed across her nape.

"And here I thought the shower this morning would tide you over," she teased, rocking back against him.

Cooper laughed and hooked his arm around her waist, turning her to face him. "When it comes to you, I've accepted the fact that I'll never get enough. You might want to try to accept it, too."

"Is that so?"

Smirking, he lifted up his beer and took a long pull.

Her brow quirked, and she shook her head. "I guess I'm lucky the feeling is mutual then."

Halle rose onto her toes and pressed her lips to his, surprising him when she deepened what he assumed would be a chaste kiss. Her tongue slipped between his lips, forcing the growl from his throat as she pressed her breasts against his chest.

The blinding urge to haul her ass up onto the counter and slide his hand between her thighs hit him like a blow to the chest. And if he thought for one second that she'd let him get away with knocking her dinner preparations to the floor to do so, he would have.

"You know," she said against his lips, "the sooner you let me finish these, the sooner we can finish what we've started." She pushed on his chest. "Now go."

"Happy Thanksgiving."

Cooper turned in time to see his mom enter the kitchen, pie in hand, and thank God, a smile on her face. He was almost used to it now, and he finally felt like he had his mom back. He still found himself holding his breath at times, waiting for the flash of the woman he'd known for the last ten years to resurface. But it never came, and he knew that had a lot to do with the woman standing next to him.

"Happy Thanksgiving, Kathryn," Halle said, taking the pie from her and putting it on the only empty spot on the table. "The pie looks beautiful, thank you. But I told you not to worry about bringing anything."

"Nonsense. Now what can I do to help?"

"Oh nothing, I've got it under—"

"You know what, Mom?" Cooper interrupted, earning a glare from Halle. "Hal was just telling me how she needs a break. You mind finishing the stuffed mushrooms?"

His mom was crossing the kitchen and washing her hands before he even finished asking the question. "Of course, you two go. I'll take over for a bit."

A defeated exhale later and Halle was untying her apron and handing it to his mom.

"Don't worry," he said when he tugged her out of the kitchen and toward the front door. "Your dinner's in good hands."

"Oh, gosh, I know that. I just wanted to make this day special for her...and you."

He paused as he was opening the door, and instead, turned around to face Halle. "You already have, baby." He glided his hand to the back of her head, then pressed a kiss to her forehead. If it wasn't for her, this house would still be as empty as it had been five months ago. No laughter, no family. She'd made his world right again.

"Besides, for Mom, it doesn't get any more special than

letting her help you."

The flecks of gold in Halle's eyes brightened as she grinned up at him. God, he loved her.

Stepping outside, the crisp autumn air was a stark contrast compared to the warmth that filled his house. As he led her to his old pickup, he could smell the scent of a distant bonfire carried by the breeze.

"I love that smell." Halle took a deep breath and released it slowly. "It reminds me of Peyton."

The familiar sting came, but it had dulled in the months since Halle returned. It was getting easier to talk about her—he was learning. He knew that ache would never truly be gone, and he didn't want it to be, either.

"It does?" he asked, pulling the tailgate down and taking a seat.

Halle sat down next to him. "Yeah. She would always beg my dad to start bonfires, knowing he could never pass up S'mores."

He laughed. "Sounds like her."

Smiling, Halle scooted back into the truck bed and lay down.

"What're you doing?" he asked, laying down next to her.

"Looking at the clouds," she said as if it were the most obvious answer. And it probably should have been. He'd watched her lay in the back of this truck when she was a kid doing the exact same thing; this had been one of her favorite games.

She burrowed into his side. He loved when they lay like this—his arm around her, her hair brushing his face, and her hand draped across his stomach. Now that he had this—it was hard to believe he'd survived so long without it, without her.

"Thank you."

"For what?" he asked.

"For pulling me away." She looked up at him. "This is just what I needed."

He kissed the top of her head and breathed in the scent of her hair. "Anytime, baby."

"So what do you see?"

He moved his gaze to the clouds above, squinting his eyes and shifting his head in different directions. Yeah... He saw clouds. "A turtle, maybe?"

"Hmm."

"I'm guessing you don't see it?"

She just laughed. "It kind of looks like a duck. What about that one over there?"

He followed her pointed finger to the clump of slowly moving clouds. "I'm going to go with a cat riding a unicycle?"

She snorted. "You're horrible at this."

Yeah, probably so. But he'd do this all day if she wanted.

"Come on," she said as she started to get up. "My time's about up. I need to check on dinner."

Cooper pulled her back into his arms. "I've still got a few more minutes."

He loved that she didn't resist him, just sighed sweetly and tangled her limbs with his as she snuggled back in to him.

"Did you feel that?" she asked.

He was feeling a lot of things at the moment, and all of them led to getting her naked, so he was trying his damnedest to ignore them.

"There it is again."

And before he could ask her what she was talking about, it was raining. The thin drizzle was coming down steady and fast, spattering them with small drops.

Halle shrieked, burying her face in his shirt, but she didn't make a move to get up. So he tightened his hold on her and crushed her against him.

The brisk wind whistled over them, and Halle shivered. Kissing her temple, he sighed. "Let's get inside, babe."

"I thought you wanted your 'few more minutes.'"

"I do, but I also want you warm."

"Then get me warm," she said, lifting her face from his chest to look up at him.

The suggestion in her eyes stirred his need—the need to taste her, the need to have her, and the overwhelming need to love her.

The rain made a sheen of mist on her skin, the fine drops rolling onto her lips. He tipped his mouth down to hers and kissed her. She whimpered, his mouth absorbing the raindrops and her pleasure as she met him with the same consuming greed he felt.

"Mmm, much better," she mumbled around their kiss.

"Good."

He felt her hand slip beneath his shirt, and he groaned as she traced his happy trail "This *is* perfect," she whispered.

His mouth stilled over hers, and she nibbled his bottom lip, coaxing him to kiss her again.

"Marry me," he said.

Her quiet gasp hung in the air. He hadn't planned it. Not that he hadn't thought about making her his wife, because he had. A lot. But the words had just come out, and now that they had, he wanted it more than anything. "Be my wife?"

When she didn't say anything, he flipped her beneath him. Her giggle relaxed the knot that had formed in his gut, but then the smile that accompanied it down right saved him.

"You want me to be your wife?" she asked, looping her arms around his neck, a soft smile turning up those heart-shaped lips he loved so much.

"I want you to be mine."

She laughed and the sound blended with falling rain around them. "I'm already yours."

Groaning, he rocked his hips against hers, his mouth finding the soft spot where her neck and shoulder curved. He licked the water from her skin, kissed her once, then whispered, "Is that a yes?"

"That's a promise."

Smiling, he skimmed his mouth across her collarbone, knowing by memory exactly where each cluster of freckles were and kissing every single one of them. "You know how much I love you?" he asked, lifting his head.

"I love you, too," she whispered.

Simultaneously, he slid off her, pulling her up with him. "I'm taking you inside."

"What?" she whined. "Now *I* want a few more minutes."

He chuckled. "Don't argue with me, baby. I'm taking my future wife inside and getting her out of these wet clothes."

Her eyes brightened with desire, her smile growing wide as she scooted off the tailgate and started toward the house. "Halle Bale," she whispered, as if saying it to herself to see how it sounded.

"You know, I saw that written about fifty times on an old sheet of paper from the keepsake box."

Pressing her lips together, she blushed and turned to look at him. "I may have scribbled it a few times that morning and snuck it in the box."

His eyebrow quirked, and she laughed.

"We'd put our dreams for the future in there," she explained, dropping his hand as she hurried up the porch.

Her steps stalled as she neared the front door, looking over her shoulder at him. Water dampened the hair that had fallen loose around her face, and her lashes spiked from the rain. She smiled at him, the one that always seemed to reach inside him and mend one of his broken pieces. He'd thought he could never be the man he used to be for her. But he was wrong.

"You coming?" she asked. "I thought you were going to take care of me and get me out of these clothes," she teased.

Without hesitation he went to her, taking the porch steps two at a time until he was close enough to draw her into his arms.

She brought her hand to the back of his head, tangling her fingers in his wet hair. "Because I was kind of hoping to get you out of your wet clothes, too."

Cocking an eyebrow, he reached around her and opened the door, then tossed her over his shoulder.

She squealed as he carried her to their room. He didn't care that their house was packed with their friends and family. He was going to take care of his future bride. His Halle.

THE END

Acknowledgments

It goes without saying that I owe an enormous thank you to my family, especially my two children. The schedule of an author is not consistent, and it's never convenient. Thanks for sticking it out with me. Love you all.

My editors, Heather Howland and Stephen Morgan, I could not have done this without you. And that's an understatement.

Heather: thank you for taking a chance on this story. I have been an Entangled fan, especially a Brazen fan, since the beginning, and to finally have the opportunity to write for the imprint is a dream come true. Thank you for making it happen. Your help and advice has been invaluable, and I feel so lucky to have worked with you.

Stephen: It has been so much fun working with you. Not only have I learned so much, but I truly felt valued as an author. The time you invested in me and my story means more to me than I can say. Thanks for the late nights (or early mornings, lol), long weekends, impromptu phone calls, and Starbucks. I can't wait to work on the next story with you!

This job would be a lonely one without my BA girls. Stacey, Tonya, Amy, Claire, and Abbi. Not only has your help and pep talks carried me through this book, but your friendship as well. I adore you girls and I'm so lucky to have you.

Gina Maxwell. You know I was a Gina fan before a Gina friend, and you are just as amazing as a person as you are a writer. I value your opinions and feedback so much, and I can't thank you enough for talking things out with me at the drop of a hat. You're the best.

I can't forget my super amazing cover models, Tayler Edson and Andrew Thomas, and my brilliant photographer, Nikki Myers. You were all such good sports, and it was so much fun. I'm so excited to have a sexy custom cover, and I couldn't be happier with the way it turned out.

I'm pretty sure I have the best agent there is. Jill Marsal: thank you, thank you, thank you.

To the many bloggers and readers that have supported me, whether they read one of my books, told a friend about my books, shared or tweeted, or simply said hi to me at an event. You all are so very important to me. Every one of you. No matter how big or how small, your support means the world. I wouldn't be here without you.

xoxo

About the Author

New York Times bestselling author Kelsie Leverich lives in Indiana with two pretty adorable monsters—who are better known as her kids—and her three little fur babies. Whether she is reading it or writing it, Kelsie is a sucker for romance. Add some toe-curling passion and she's done for. When not writing, she can usually be found behind the chair at the salon, or out on the lake with friends and family. Kelsie is a lipstick junkie, nail polish hoarder, and lover of words. She is most definitely not a morning person, has a soft spot for animals, loves musicals, hates seafood, and thinks laundry is the source of all evil.

www.kelsieleverich.com